T0035576

LOST
ARK
DREAMING

ALSO BY SUYI DAVIES OKUNGBOWA

THE NAMELESS REPUBLIC

Son of the Storm

Warrior of the Wind

David Mogo, Godhunter

LOST ARK DREAMING

Suyi Davies Okungbowa

Tor Publishing Group
New York

LOST ARK DREAMING

A Tordotcom Book
Published by Tom Doherty Associates / Tor Publishing Group
120 Broadway
New York, NY 10271

www.torpublishinggroup.com

Tor® is a registered trademark of Macmillan Publishing Group, LLC.

Library of Congress Cataloging-in-Publication Data

Names: Okungbowa, Suyi Davies, author.
Title: Lost ark dreaming / Suyi Davies Okungbowa.
Description: First edition. | New York : Tor Publishing Group, 2024.
Identifiers: LCCN 2024002433 | ISBN 9781250890757 (hardcover) |
    ISBN 9781250890764 (ebook)
Subjects: LCGFT: Apocalyptic fiction. | Climate fiction. | Novellas.
Classification: LCC PR9387.9.O394327 L67 2024 | DDC 823/.92—dc23/
    eng/20240117
LC record available at https://lccn.loc.gov/2024002433

Our books may be purchased in bulk for promotional, educational, or business use. Please contact your local bookseller or the Macmillan Corporate and Premium Sales Department at 1-800-221-7945, extension 5442, or by email at MacmillanSpecialMarkets@macmillan.com.

First Edition: 2024

Printed in the United States of America

0 9 8 7 6 5 4 3 2 1

For Lucy Kirkman and Aurelie Sheehan:
rest gentle and easy.

LOST
ARK
DREAMING

WHAT ARE WE BUT WATER AND SKIN?

My dearest All-Infinite—

You must understand
that this is the way
the world always ends:

    in

worthy questions
left unanswered
    lonely
hearts and empty eyes;

lapping warnings
nightly silence
    ripples
in the undersea.

YEKINI

Yekini had one dream, and the ark was always in it.

She had never been religious—not in the old ways before the deluge, not in the new way of the master clerics, and not in the way of those who secretly tended to bygone spiritualities. Yekini should never have even known the tale of the ark and the flood. But somewhere between tower-wide broadcasts regaling denizens with sermons about the fulfillment of the Second Deluge, and Maame—who *was* intensely spiritual and knew too many tales from above and under the sea—learning about it was inevitable.

The dream was always the same. The ark's keeper stood at the bow in a flowing robe, reaching out, asking Yekini to hand over the basket. Sometimes, it was Olókun who stood there, stretching forth a tentacle. Sometimes, it was Noah, with a bushy beard and a tight squint, crow's-feet at the edge of his eyes. Other times it was Sekhmet in her lioness head, or Uta-napishtim looking like immortality personified, or Deucalion or Waynaboozhoo or Manu. Sometimes, the ark was a boat or a ship or a raft.

Regardless of who stood there or on what, Yekini always looked down, into the face of the baby in the basket.

The baby was her—or at least had her face. Sometimes, the face was that of her foster grandfather, Maame's husband—an approximation, since he passed before Yekini was three. Sometimes, it was what she imagined her own parents would've looked like if they'd survived long enough for her infant brain to retain their features. Sometimes, it was a friend, a colleague, an acquaintance. Always someone she could choose to save.

The real problem was that she always chose not to.

The ark's keeper would try to collect the basket from her, but she would hold on, fingers locked in a vise grip, knuckles taut. Halfway through this tug-of-war, her awareness would return, and she would see that they were not standing on the deck of the ark or boat or raft, but on the roof of the Pinnacle, overlooking the other four towers of the Fingers—back when they were still beacons of radiant hope, long before they fell and became derelict. Except, this wasn't the Fingers, but Old Lagos from the time before the waters, how she'd seen the city portrayed in media feeds.

And just when she thought of that, the waters would come.

The wind always arrived first, tickling her eyebrows, and when she looked down, the waters would rise, rise, without warning, as the reports had said they did. One moment, yellow automobiles plied the streets far below; next moment, they floated on their sides alongside everything else: trees, buildings, people. She would look up and realize the ark was not the ark at all, but a rescue helicopter, taking off with the ark's keeper staring out the window, shaking their head as they left her standing there with the basket. The basket, which, when she looked down, was now empty, lacking answers yet filled with questions.

Then she would wake up in a sweat and realize she was late for work.

Today, for instance.

0730, Day 262, Year 059 the glowing numbers on her nightstand read, which meant she was on the morning rota, which meant she was due at work in half an hour, which meant she had slept through her alarm—which meant her dreams were becoming more intense.

Yekini scrambled out of bed, slammed her knee into the built-in nightstand and cursed. She crawled to the kitchen, put a dishcloth under the spigot, squeezed, and wiped her armpits and privates. Next: a breath mint. Between cleaning teeth and dressing up, there was only time for one.

When the pain in her knee subsided, she slid the wardrobe open, moisturized her locs and palm-rolled those closest to her face while picking out a clean suit. Midder dress code for work was pastels, and she went for a quick and efficient gray and white. She was halfway through stepping into her shoes when she heard Maame's raspy breathing from the living room.

Shit.

Yekini hopped to the kitchen and programmed a breakfast sequence for her grandmother. As the pot confirmed prep settings for corn pap, she popped her head around the doorway to see if the woman was awake. Dim light washed over Maame from the screen she'd been watching the night before, but her chair was still reclined to its sleep position, her eyes still shut.

Yekini whispered the remaining instructions to the unit's assistant: *Shut off screen, set timed lights, set alarms for Maame's medication, set alarms for Maame's programs.* The assistant whispered back its confirmation. Satisfied, Yekini slipped out the door and whispered her final instructions for a timed lock.

The hallway outside was like most Pinnacle corridors: wide and curved. Yekini ran for the elevators, often not seeing oncoming pedestrians until she'd almost bumped into them. It took her a while to realize she was on the southbound track. She crossed quickly to the outer northbound track, to the dismay of a tram driver who almost careened into her. No time to apologize. She had to make the elevators.

She arrived just in time to catch the last one, slipping in before the doors closed, breathing heavily, sweat lining her neck. The car advanced upward, packed full of midders like her who worked so high up the tower that their shoulders almost brushed the Uppers. Most were dressed in the same way as she—essential, minimalist—making it clear they also worked in some arm of government.

They shot her glances anyway. Perhaps today it was the sweat and her slightly rumpled clothes. But it could just as easily have been the blotch of yellow dye in the corner of her hair, or the fancy pin on her suit. She enjoyed a dash of color every now and then. Her coworkers and superiors, like most midders, did not.

Once the car eased into level 66 and the doors opened, Yekini shot down the corridor, glancing at her wearable every few seconds. *0756, 0758, 0759.* At 0800, she crossed the sign that said COMMISSION FOR THE PROTECTION OF THE FINGERS.

A grid of workstations, laid out over the large floor, welcomed her into the agency. She scurried through them to the workzone in the rear that read ANALYSTS, one eye on the clock. Her station, all the way in the back row where junior analysts sat, was within reach. She raced to her desk and pressed her finger onto the station scanner, clocking in. The desk pinged its acceptance and began to process. Yekini crossed her fingers, counting the seconds, wishing for a miracle.

The desk pinged. *You Have Arrived,* it congratulated her. *0801 hours.*

"Fuck me," said Yekini, slumping into the chair.

She leaned her head back over the headrest, waiting for a second ping, one that was *definitely* going to be bad news. Sure enough, before her thought was complete, the desk pinged one more time. Yekini sighed, tapped the screen, read the message, then frowned.

This was a mistake, surely? She'd only been a minute late this time—that didn't warrant this kind of response. And yes, her punctuality strikes had racked up, blah blah blah, but . . . something was wrong here. Something had to be.

Because why on Savior's given waters would they send her *undersea?*

YEKINI

"Undersea?" a voice said from behind Yekini. "Aha, aha!"

Monsignor was an analyst with square shoulders and droopy lips, stationed opposite Yekini's desk. He began to clap, whistling, yelling, "Undersea! Undersea!"

Others in the workzone joined in. It wasn't every day someone got sent below surface—once or twice a year, maybe. Privilege or punishment—it could be either. This was a task that had to be earned, either by racking up good deeds, making terrible gaffes, or both.

Monsignor goaded his coworkers, turning to Yekini to do the honors. Typically, the agent in question would show good comradeship by offering a mock bow, indulging everyone.

Yekini was not a good comrade.

"Sit down," she hissed. Monsignor complied grudgingly. The applause petered out.

"You *did* ask for a solo field assignment," he said.

"Yeah, but *undersea* for my first?" She shook her head, staring at the message. "That's not . . ."

"Routine? Coincidence?" Monsignor turned the seat around and straddled it, arms folded across the backrest. "Yeah, no. You must've pissed somebody off. Makes sense if they decided your first solo be down in the Lowers. Teach you a bit of a lesson."

Yekini glared at Monsignor, but she knew he was right. Even senior analysts with proper butt-in-chair and hands-on-station time didn't go out into the field much, and fewer still went below surface. She'd progressed quickly enough to be considered for six field assignments since joining the Commission three years ago, but had been rejected for them all. Midder assignments, too, those ones. This was a whole new level. Literally.

"I didn't piss anyone off," Yekini said, more to herself than Monsignor, who was now taking a mint from the bowl on her desk. She shot him a hard side-eye and he put it back reluctantly, pushing her screen aside to get a clearer view of her face.

"Congratulations either way. Shey they say those who go below surface are the hardboiled ones? Maybe being elevated from desk junkie straight to field agent is more blessing than curse. Girl, be happy."

Yekini pulled her screen back to its former position. Monsignor, finally sensing her irritation, swiveled his chair away. She turned to her screen, swiping the message to and fro, bringing it in and out of view, as if she could glean more meaning each time she looked at it anew.

"Better stop swiping and go prep," Monsignor said without turning. "If you have any query, talk to Timipre before you go."

Yekini stared some more before taking Monsignor's advice. She strode down the hallway, to the office door that said DIRECTOR: MERIT TIMIPRE. The door was locked and there was no light at the bottom.

Well, then. Talking to the director would have to wait. One hour left before mobilization, and she knew what she'd rather spend it on. She needed to gather as much information as possible about the Lowers, and get the resources required for the trip from Storage.

Luckily for her, there was one person who could guide her through both.

"Undersea," Nabata said, and whistled.

"You people are overdoing the melodrama at this rate."

"What can I say? I'm not sure whether to congratulate you or tell you sorry."

"Just process my order and let me know what's up."

Nabata, small and lively and always in one form of headdress or another—today it was a turban—swung the half door that said EQUIPMENT STORAGE STAFF ONLY and angled her head for Yekini to follow.

They went together into the massive warehouse. Metal shelves ran screed to ceiling in the multi-floor area. Drones zipped about on errands, scanning, grabbing, offloading, restocking. The two women headed for the nearest request station, accessible via a metal gangway. Nabata thumbed it, and Yekini punched in her assignment code. The list of required protective equipment for her assignment came onscreen: *helmet, lightweight capped boots with suction grip, body armor with inflatable lining, firearm.*

"Savior above," Yekini said. "A *firearm*?"

"It's the Lowers, madam," Nabata said. "You know what they say: prepare for anything."

Yekini snickered. "*They.* As if you aren't one of them doing the saying."

Nabata held her hands up in mock denial. "I can neither confirm nor deny that I've ever used such words."

They double-checked the list to be sure they had everything.

"I haven't even held a firearm since boot camp," Yekini said. "And I know my oga at the top has been very particular about ammunition being limited."

"They must really need you to go down there, hmm?"

"Apparently. But *why*?"

Nabata shrugged. "You *did* say you wanted—"

"—a field job, yes I know, you people can stop reminding me."

Nabata laughed. "Sorry. Architect of your own misfortune."

They sent off the order. The station chimed its approval, and a drone whirred up somewhere and started off on the errand.

"It's true you've been wasting behind that station, though," said Nabata. "But then, you also have stronghead, and it shows, even in your correspondence. Someone definitely wants this to be a mindfuck."

"Yeah." What Yekini didn't say was that somewhere within her, something even stronger than her own will, antsier than her own nerves, was pushing, pushing, pushing. Showing up in her dreams. It was not by choice that she'd wanted to get out of that chair. It was a force to which she had no choice but to succumb.

"Undersea no bad reach like that, though," Nabata said. "Everyone just talks about it as if people go there to die. I mean, I was born and raised there. Am I dead?"

The two women had met at a Commission-wide Midder event and bonded over a shared contempt for the way Pinnacle citizens spoke about the below surface. Especially after they'd had a drink too many, and their teeth had given up gating their disdain. Yekini had a particular bone to pick with the midders who lived on the very last above-sea level, those who could look outside and see the water surface right there—even *they* had the gall to talk shit about those living undersea.

Nabata had crawled her way up to the lowest levels of the Midders by luck—she had won the migration lottery and was now one of those lucky enough to work for the Commission. *Liberated from the depths of undersea,* as the Office of the Pinnacle Leadership would say in tower-wide broadcasts. At the party, the two women had carved out a corner of the room and taken to bashing their haughtier colleagues. There was a lot of laughing, possibly helped by the fact that they, too, had been plied with drink.

Their shared values eventually blossomed into friendship. Most COPOF agents and analysts didn't engage much with the backroom staff, but Yekini considered Nabata someone she could count as an ally in the Commission, and to Nabata she was a breath of fresh air compared to other midder workers. It was difficult enough trying to make it as young women in an agency dominated by men. Support from anyone at all was cherished.

The inventory drone arrived with a bag of equipment and dropped it before them. Yekini opened it and checked for completeness. She pulled out the firearm and its holster, inspecting them: a COPOF-issue quick-burst model. She checked the ammunition chamber and flicked the safety, just to see. It looked like it worked fine.

"Want to test it at the range?" Nabata asked. "You don't want to go down there and find it's not working."

"For someone from undersea, you hold a very healthy opinion of the Lowers."

Nabata laughed. "We're like those old vampire films from the 2000s—the ones they show on the screens sometimes? We hug you, warmly, but we also bite your neck."

Yekini had always found it a contradiction that Nabata referred to the lowers as *we,* even though she was a midder now, yet referenced the physical place as *down there,* reinforcing her distance from it. And yet, Yekini understood this dissonance perfectly. Maame and Granpa had been classified lowers as children, but had found a way to ascend for the sake of their children—Yekini's parents. At least, that was the story Maame told, and that explained why Maame herself still sometimes said *we* when talking about the lowers in this tower.

Maame and Granpa had been lowers in another tower, where Yekini's parents had been born, right before each tower began to fail, one after the other, until all became the decrepit and empty shells they were now, except for the Pinnacle. The survivors all had to move somewhere, Maame and family included. It was how they'd found themselves as refugees in the Pinnacle, beginning the painstaking work of rebuilding their lives, piece by piece, level by level.

Maame and Granpa, that is. Yekini's parents did not make it over.

"I think everywhere has its vampires," Yekini said, sorting through the rest of the equipment. "We up here in the Midders bite too. We've never been to the Uppers, but I bet they do just as much, if not even more."

They packed the bag and returned to the storeroom front.

"Stop worrying." Nabata locked the half door as Yekini exited. "Just mind your business, and you'll be fine. If there's one thing about the lowers, it's that we know how to mind our business. Just because we live undersea doesn't mean we're as bad as the terrors living in the waters themselves."

"Stop saying *we*," Yekini said. "You're a midder now."

"Ha," said Nabata. "Remind your colleagues. They pretend not to know that."

Yekini blew her a kiss, then left for mobilization.

WHAT ARE WE BUT STORIES THAT TOUCH?

All-Knowing, my friend—

Once upon a time—because this is the way all real stories begin, yes?—Sister Sea stayed far, far away, in her own place. And Brother Land—he sat just so, right where he was. And all was well with that world, because all knew that one may choose for a people, but one does not *choose* for Land—or worse, for Sea.

Water no get enemy, so who dares make an enemy of Her?

Now see, there were those who Have and those who Did Not Have. They fashioned elegant words for this false arrangement, called them things like *nations.* And those who Have—for all they did was *have* and *choose*—chose to have what they couldn't.

This, friend, is the way the world always ends, has always ended since we have watched it together: with those who Have choosing demise—*always* demise—for everything but themselves.

Entry #D-2292

Start of excerpt.

PROPERTY PRO MONTHLY

Diekara Goes Skyward

*Africa's Biggest Real Estate Mogul Bets
on High-Rise Living Communities*

by Brenda Alli

2 February 2034

When we think of skyscrapers and high-rises in Lagos, we think of mega-corporate entities like banks and financial organizations, oil-and-gas companies, professional service firms, hotels and the hospitality business, malls and entertainment. We do not think of our children riding their bicycles on purpose-designed trails in the halls of a high-rise, or public tramcars riding beside them. We do not think about everything we associate with a home: great cooking, holiday decorations, school runs. But that is what Chief Akanni Diekara Sr., owner and CEO of Diekara Industries Limited, the biggest real estate family business south of the Sahara, is thinking about.

"Making home in the heights is the future of luxury," he says, as he takes me on a tour ahead of the grand opening of his newest project, the smallest of five towers he has named the Diekara Atlantic Community.

We're standing in the mid-level concourse on the fiftieth floor of the smallest tower, which is nearly a hundred floors. Around us are silent, yet-to-be-opened spaces that will house commercial enterprises in the coming months: banking, supermarkets, pharmacies, electronics and hardware stores, fitness centers, beauty salons, restaurants, even a community swimming pool. Signs are already up in anticipation.

The DAC is a nifty little project. It sticks out of a private island—man-made with sand dredged up from the bottom of the ocean—that's far enough from shore to require a boat trip, but close enough that the five towers can be seen from the beach, sticking out of the ocean like a lonely hand. The locals have nicknamed it *Awọn Ika*, meaning *the*

Fingers. The title has gained momentum in both colloquial and official usage, with locals even going so far as to name each tower by its position on the "hand."

Our current tower is called *Little.* The others, still at the foundations-and-scaffolding stage, will go by similar monikers once completed: *Thumb, Index, Fourth.* The tallest of them all—expected to be completed by 2050 and planned to reach 180 levels (over a *kilometer* high)—will be an outlier. It will go by *Pinnacle.*

"The price is right," Diekara says, when I bring up the ongoing public concern about the prohibitive cost of securing a spot on his towers. "No product is ever meant for everybody—we have a target market."

He talks me through construction. I'm a journalist, not an engineer, so I only follow the phrases of interest and impact. *State-of-the-art self-contained housing units. In-built home and office assistant technology. Underwater electricity-generating turbines. Flood-proof levels, up to a third of each tower's height above sea level.*

I ask him why Diekara Industries is so invested in preparing for a submerged future. Does he think his island will be swallowed soon?

"Swallowed?" He laughs. "Listen, this is a project built to last generations, centuries. So, yes, we need to prepare for all possible futures, including one of submergence. But that's not for us here to worry about, no. It's for those *over there.*"

We're standing at one of the expansive windows of the concourse. I follow his arm, pointing at the rugged cityscape of Lagos that stares back at us. This high up, the economic stratification is quite evident to any keen eye. Rusted-zinc slums already half-submerged by rising floods stand next to glittering apartment buildings that sport paved elevated roadways, sidestepping the rapidly rising waters like a disgusted foot.

"Nobody wants to live in that impending chaos," Diekara says. "Everyone will fight to come up here when that is no more. They will stand in that same spot you're standing and say, *Thanks to Diekara, we escaped.*"

End of excerpt.

NGOZI

To Ngozi Nwafor, *early* was another word for *sufferhead*. Early risers, early meetings, early tasks—he detested them all. The one benefit of being a mid-level administrator in the Office of the Pinnacle Leadership was that he didn't have to work *that* hard. Not like other tower citizens, at least—excepting Pinnacle leadership, of course, whose only job was to exist (and he did not have a problem with that at all).

And yet, Ngozi prided himself on doing just that little bit more than most of his colleagues. A blessing and a curse. For one, it kept him top-of-mind with his superiors, especially OPL Deputy Director Kelechi Azubuike. Sooner or later, Ngozi was bound to be a senior administrator himself.

But it was also the very reason he was now standing in the express speedcar reserved for OPL officials, shooting down a hundred levels. That same diligence had likely gotten him this early-morning, runt-of-the-litter task. Imagine, a whole OPL administrator going undersea just to debrief an engineer for triggering a breach alert.

Blessing-curse. That had to be his middle name.

"Rubbish," he said to the empty cubicle, the speedcar's whirring the only sound about him. "Somebody must've told Azubuike to *Give it to Ngozi. He's the OPL messenger boy. He will do it, no questions asked.*"

He absentmindedly slipped a hand between his shirt's buttons, pulled out the pendant of his necklace and massaged it. The pendant's clear glass reflected the speedcar's lights, ghost glints chasing one another. Ensconced within the pendant was a flash of color, the only valuable part of the necklace—a small remnant of an aged, wrinkled orange peel.

"If not for you," Ngozi whispered to the orange peel, then

tucked it back into his shirt, gazing at his own dour expression in the speedcar's doors.

The car stopped at a level and the door opened, bringing him out of his reverie. A young man dressed in the same gray OPL-worker-issue suit as Ngozi was—tie and shirt and everything—stood at the door. He hesitated when he noticed Ngozi's expression.

"Please enter if you're entering, don't be wasting my time," Ngozi said.

The young man looked unsure. Ngozi sucked his teeth and waved at the sensor. The man walked away. The doors shut.

Ngozi returned to glaring at the reflective doors. That lackadaisical engineer did not think whose morning they'd be ruining by sending that nonsense critical alert, did they? *An undersea breach*—by what, an octopus? A ghost? A Child? Caused a mini-panic in the office—all for what? *Rubbish.*

The speedcar stopped at level 66, where he was meant to pick up the COPOF agent assigned to accompany him to the Lowers. When the door opened, he expected to see a bodyguard-type person. Instead, a young woman dressed in protective equipment came in. She was slight, wore locs, and did not at all look like what he expected of a COPOF agent—or a tower official for that matter. She carried a bag, and a firearm was strapped to her hip.

"Excuse me," he said, "I think you have the wrong car."

"Oh, no," the woman said, looking around. "I think I have it right. Ngozi Nwafor, I presume?"

He tapped his wearable and pulled up the info sent across. Sure enough, it was her—*Yekini, Yekini: Rank I Analyst, Commission for the Protection of the Fingers*. The photo looked exactly like she did, but with different hair—plaits.

"Huh," he said. "It says here you're an analyst."

She stepped into the elevator. "I am."

"So they sent me a novice for a field mission?" He laughed, and it was harsh and acerbic. "This is really good morning to you, Ngozi."

"I have all the necessary training to accompany you to the Lowers, Mr. Nwafor."

"I can't even deal with this right now." He waved at the doors, shutting them, then motioned to the bag in her hand. "What's that?"

"UPE—undersea protective equipment," she said. "For you."

"I'm not wearing that."

"It's protocol, Mr. Nwafor," she said, her tone taking on an edge, but her expression remaining cool. "We are not allowed to go undersea without protective equipment."

"These filthy things? That you all have been in?"

Yekini leaned forward and waved at the doors. The speedcar slowed its descent.

"Listen, sir," the woman said slowly, as if speaking to a child. "You will wear this, or I will get out of this elevator, and you will go undersea alone. Then I will file *my* report about how I refused to endanger the life of an OPL official. How about that?"

Ngozi grunted, grabbed the bag from her and pulled out the kit. The descriptions read like armor: *helmet, steel-toe boots, tactical vest.* Okay, they *were* armor. They were also heavy, damp and smelled of mold, as he'd expected. When he put them on, it felt like he was going to war.

The more he thought about it, maybe he was.

They reached level 32, the last above-surface level—at least depending on the tides. Sometimes it was level 33 or 34. The speedcar stopped whirring and they got out and crossed the tiny lobby to another elevator reserved for government officials. This one was bulky and spacious and stoutly built, and though Ngozi did not know what it was called, he knew, by the way the doors clanged shut, iron against iron, that this one did not have speed-anything before its name.

The heavy elevator sank to the Lowers in slow motion.

YEKINI

The smell was the first thing Yekini noted once the doors opened. The Lowers smelled like a damp cloth that had been locked in a steel box for years. It hit her full-on as they emerged onto a wide entryway—a main street of sorts.

The difference in air pressure was next. The whole tower, undersea included, maintained surface pressure to avoid inhabitants getting decompression sickness while moving between levels. Despite that, the air weighed a ton, and Yekini's lungs worked hard to draw it in. Her chest felt waterlogged, like a bad cough brewing. Her ears popped. Goose bumps spread out over her skin, paper-thin and sensitive.

And then, the darkness.

Yekini was used to not seeing the sun for stretches of time. Much of the Pinnacle's Midder zone had been constructed with a smattering of portholes, in anticipation of a possible future Third Deluge. Light diffusers and virtual sunshine screens abounded in lieu, and though they were no substitute for the real thing—the *light* was there, but the *heat* was missing—Yekini could get by with them. If she ever needed the real sun, she could simply see it through the ports of certain offices at the agency, like Director Merit's.

But down here, the darkness was different. Though the lights were bright and functional, she couldn't shake the feeling of being surrounded by an *endless* night. One power cut, and they would all plunge into the blackness of the deep. The thought of such a possibility caused bile to rise up to her throat and stay there.

A migration desk welcomed them, blocking their path. A young man, dressed in the unmistakable red and white of a police uniform, sat behind it. He wasn't armed, but the few other police personnel standing strategically about were.

"Entry passes," he said, not looking up.

"Biochip or wearable?" asked Yekini.

"Chip."

Yekini and Ngozi took off their wearables and presented the chips embedded in their forearms to be scanned. The man looked at his screens for a second, then up at the two and their gear. He had a slight frown of worry, especially glancing at Yekini's firearm.

"Expecting trouble?" he asked her.

"Hopefully not," she squeaked. Her voice had become higher-pitched, due to the greater air density.

"Follow the signs," he said, and pointed them in a direction.

She and Ngozi put their wearables back on and went where the signs said, taking them to the series of elevators that connected to the lower levels. They got into a nearby elevator and went down to level 9. No one else got in or rode with them. Yekini's ears popped various times as they descended. She pulled out chewing putty, offering Ngozi one. He shook his head and opted to make funny faces to get the air out of his ears.

"Did you really need to bring that along?" Ngozi asked, gesturing toward her firearm.

"It was in the equipment requirements."

Ngozi shook his head. "We might as well be police. Let's hope anybody will talk to us at this rate."

The smell intensified—or at least in Yekini's mind—when they stepped into level 9. It looked as nondescript as the one they'd just left, likely because they had emerged at the work wing. Everyone who went past them seemed to be dressed in a uniform of some sort—coveralls, mostly—and those who weren't bore a brisk, businesslike strut. The glaring absence of police and the visibly decrepit state of the decor ensured that this place would definitely not at all be mistaken for a Midder level.

There was another migration check-in point—a large screen, this time. Ngozi inputted the name of the person they were here to see: the level foreman, Tuoyo Odili. The screen offered them directions to a suggested meeting point.

Ngozi downloaded the directions into his wearable, and they went on. Workers milled about, mostly ignoring them, heads down and focused on the floor, or up and focused only forward, or in groups and only focused on themselves. But the farther they went, the more out of place Yekini started to feel, and the more noticeable the two of them became.

It was not simply their gear, she could tell. It could've been anything else: their squared shoulders, set back with assurance, like people who believed they belonged wherever they went; or their obviously better-tended skin from the good air and water upside compared to the paler, vitamin-D-deficient lowers; or the fact that she wore locs when every single person of any gender down here had their hair cut short. Each passerby took one look at them both and immediately *knew* that they were midders.

With these stares came understanding, and with understanding came what Yekini first interpreted to be hostility, as her agency-trained mind was wont to do—and her fingers rested on her holster for a moment—before she recognized it for what it was: *disdain*.

Not *hate*—at least, not in the way the agency had taught her that it existed between tower citizens and everything else out there. Here, she and Ngozi were unlikely to be harmed. Spat upon, maybe, but not violently assaulted. Lowers simply did not want to see them at all if they could help it.

"It's like rats live down here," Ngozi muttered, loud enough so that those who went by could hear. A person or two looked back at them, but Ngozi held his head high, and Yekini had never been more ashamed than she was in that moment.

TUOYO

Tuoyo's day had begun with a literal bang. A junior technician woke her up by slamming repeatedly on her unit door rather than doing the respectable thing and pinging her ahead of arrival. But all expectation of etiquette vanished when he revealed that something had torn a hole in the airlock of level 9, and as level foreman and head of safety, it was her duty to see to it.

First things first: she sent a sitrep upstairs, labeled it *critical* as protocol demanded. Then she reported at the desk long before her shift was due.

Turned out the culprit was a broken panel in the sluice gates used to flood the airlock for underwater exits, an action they hadn't carried out in a while. A broken gate meant they couldn't deflood and depressurize the airlock, the one thing it was good for.

The hole in question was a split seam in the airlock's wall. Tuoyo guessed that sustained underwater pressure on the aging walls must've done it. They were lucky this was a level where the walls were fortified, meaning there was no structural damage. This was also a work wing and not a residential one, so the leak had only affected a few isolated areas and some engineering equipment.

She quickly dispatched two teams: a cleanup crew to seal off the wet areas of the tower and begin siphoning the water, and a tech team to the airlock to repair the gate and mend the seam. In the interim, she spent an hour peering over sweaty heads at various monitors with feeds from the Pinnacle's exterior underwater cameras.

There was no sign of any NTD—*non-tower dweller,* as the OPL classified them. No sign of a breach on the outside walls either. The sluice gate's break was clean along the edge, so it didn't look like the work of an external party. Constant pressure changes could do that to aged material. She'd noticed such weaknesses in other parts of the level, so it wasn't far-fetched. The Lowers were built shitty anyways, a situation she found surprising for people as smart as uppers supposedly were. Didn't they know that if the Lowers crumbled, the whole tower would follow?

She watched from the monitors as the techs replaced the broken gate, then returned to the airlock and began to weld the split seam. It was really one errant wall panel, and took about an hour to fix. Afterward, they deflooded and depressurized the airlock, checked for leaks, pressurized and flooded it again just to be sure.

Everything seemed fine.

As the team waited in the chamber for the final deflooding and depressurization cycle, Tuoyo sent a follow-up sitrep upstairs with copious notes about cause, damage and repairs. She removed the critical warning she'd initially appended to the report. Hopefully, upstairs hadn't dispatched a response yet— and even if they had, she could defend her decision. A seam split in the walls *was* critical.

One hour left until her shift ended. She retired to her workroom to catch a bit of sweet sleep, and was just about dozing off when she was awakened, rudely, by the beeping of her handheld.

She rose from the pull-out cot in the tiny workroom and peered at the screen. A visit: two officials from the Midders were on their way to see her with regard to the breach.

Ugh. Protocol would be the death of her.

Then she saw the designation of the officials, and her heart began to beat a little bit faster. The last time someone from CO-POF had shown up to see her, it was for a very different reason. The dark cloud that hung over her life had formed that day and had not left since.

Breathe, Tuoyo. Breathe.

She pushed the bleak thoughts down and folded the cot back into its compartment. As she squeezed back into her jumpsuit, she swiped through their profiles, wondering why the COPOF would send someone. Did they think this was an internal *threat*? Or worse, external?

Did they think it was *Children*?

The thought of Children sent a chill through her, fear braided with antipathy. She pushed it down.

She met them in the hallway. They were dressed funny, their protective getup a mixed bag between high-risk conflict and underwater gear, but completely neither.

"Are you the foreman for this level?" the short man asked without pleasantries. Tuoyo was immediately reminded why she hated being in the same room with these Midder government types.

"Good day to you too," she said, her demeanor flat. "I'm Tuoyo Odili, level nine supervisor for HSE and Security."

"I'm Yekini," the woman next to him said, and waved awkwardly.

"Yes, yes," the man—profile name: Ngozi—said impatiently. "Can we get this done?"

Tuoyo led them down the corridors to the south end of the level, what she liked to think of as the aft of the Pinnacle. The tower itself was almost shaped like the old ships of yore—or like many such ships stacked one atop the other. The south face was the stern, and the north face the bow—which was why her mind thought of it as the Pinnacle's forward. It was a marvelous feat of engineering and architecture, and if not for the challenging conditions of the Lowers, amidst other life challenges, she might've even loved living here.

"Why are you dressed like that?" she asked the officials. They looked at each other, confused.

"The mobilization brief said this is how we should gear up," Yekini said. She was a young woman—younger than Tuoyo, at least—slightly impish, and gave off the impression that she regarded all of this as some sort of novelty.

"Oh," said Tuoyo. "So, you fell for the prank, then."

Ngozi frowned. "The *what*?"

"Your people do it all the time. Because you lot never come

down here, they tell you that you need all these ridiculous things. See if you'll know." She eyed Yekini's firearm. "You don't need that for anything here, unless you're trying to start some disturbance. Or you're police. Or both."

"I knew it," said Ngozi, slapping his palms. He turned to Yekini. "You know your superior will be hearing from me, yes?"

Yekini seemed to have something on the tip of her tongue, but opted not to speak it. They went on in silence.

"You sound very erudite," said Ngozi. "I was led to believe that lowers aren't very, well, sound."

"Mr. *Nwafor*," Yekini said.

"What? It's just a question."

Just a question. Tuoyo snorted.

"Something funny?"

"Yes," said Tuoyo. "You. You are funny." She said *funny* like *idiot,* and hoped it was obvious to any discerning ear, Ngozi's included.

"Explain." He said it like a command, an attempt to claw back some of his splattered dignity. Tuoyo didn't want to fall for it, but decided he needed the lesson.

"*Just a question,*" she repeated. "People like you say things like that so you don't have to face the truth about yourselves." He made to interject, so she hastily added: "And before you say it's not true, I *know* it is because I used to live in the Midders."

That gave him pause, and she proceeded.

"People told me things like this throughout my time up there. They thought they were being nice. I don't know what your definition of *nice* is, but implying that everyone is stupid where I come from doesn't sound nice to me. And, if you must know, many lowers are very well educated, myself included. You think this tower is held up by the Savior's hands?"

Ngozi, who seemed to have tuned out a while back, suddenly snapped his fingers. "I knew it!"

The two women glanced at each other. Yekini made a disdainful click in the back of her tongue.

"And what did you *knew*?" Tuoyo said dryly.

"Your name," said Ngozi. "It sounded familiar."

Oh no.

"You're *that* Tuoyo Odili," he was saying. "That was your wife, right? The anthropologist who was all over the screens a few years ago—she was on that boat expedition that was attacked by Children?"

Tuoyo swallowed. Though she had long left that midder life behind, every now and again she ran into someone who recognized her from the family photos of her and Nehikhare that had filled the broadcasts. The OPL had put them up without her consent, of course, trying desperately to turn eyes toward the stories of the people lost, and away from the actual cause of the disaster.

She'd hated talking about it then, and she hated talking about it now. She'd spoken about it enough for a lifetime.

"I'm sorry for your loss," Yekini said.

Tuoyo nodded. "It was a long time ago."

"So you know about Children, then?" Ngozi said, oblivious. "Tell us—do you think it's Children, this breach?"

She did not think it was Children. She did not think it was anything. She did not think at all. She wanted to stop talking.

"Children can't survive out of water" was all she could offer.

"Ah," said Ngozi. "Of course. I knew that."

The airlock's heavy doors came into view. Tuoyo breathed a sigh of relief and punched in the entry code.

The airlock looked and smelled exactly like it did after every flooding—dank and moldy. It used to be re-insulated periodically, but like most things in the Lowers, that had not been done in a long time. Rust had now taken over the place and it looked more derelict than it should have. Light came from a single source: a large lamp at the sealed exit.

The most alien thing here was the sea gunk that stuck around after every flooding, and the smell that came with it. Some of it was possessions from a life before, things that did not degrade, mostly plastic. Some of it was the nondegradable parts of un-recognizable gear, industrial and building material from whatever structures still stood, buried under the new sea level. Most of it was litter—container caps, cosmetic products with the names washed off. They clung to the walls like starfish.

Tuoyo remembered how fascinated Nehikhare used to be by this trash. *Not trash,* as she'd say. *A window into life in the olden days.* Every now and then, there would be knickknacks from said olden days in their unit—a personal item recovered on an expedition, a portion of a piece of equipment, some sand dug up from the seabed that used to be Old Lagos. Tuoyo hated it then, and as was her way, had been vocal about her distaste. But Nehikhare would laugh it off and kiss her, and then Tuoyo would forget how to make words.

Ngozi coughed. It echoed in the metal chamber.

"My ears." He poked a finger in each ear and twisted.

"You get used to it," Tuoyo said.

"I don't know how you can. Smells like fish in here." He surveyed the compartment. "If this is just a transition chamber between us and outside, why is a broken sluice a critical problem again?"

"The critical alert wasn't for the sluice," she said, pointing to the newly repaired section along the wall edge. "It was for *that.*"

The weld lines were so clean they would've been unnoticeable if not for existing rust. Tuoyo marveled, for a moment, at how neat it all was, how much good training she'd imparted to the techs.

"Okay, but I'm still struggling to see how that's critical. It's just leakage, right?"

It wasn't a bad question—not from a non-engineer, at least. But she found herself swallowing a scoff at *just leakage.* This man and his *justs.*

"We have a saying down here: *every leak is death,*" she replied. "Maybe for you up there, a leak only means a failure of plumbing. But down here, an unattended leak could easily mean a *structural* failure. A leak here is bad for all of us." She leaned in, hoping to drive home her message. *"All of us."*

"Okay, wow, you're an intense woman," Ngozi said, recoiling.

Yekini, who had been pacing around the airlock so far, poking her head into corners and peering at edges, had stopped at the sluice gate and was inspecting the repairs. Without looking at the others, she said: "That split looks bigger than I expected."

Tuoyo was unsure how to respond to that.

"Unless they welded beyond the hole." Yekini's expression had shifted from impish to serious. "Because that looks almost big enough—"

"To fit a person," Tuoyo completed, and she suddenly wasn't so sure what she believed had happened anymore.

"I thought you said it was pressure?" Ngozi asked, but Yekini was already moving. She approached the weld, ran her fingers down the lines, then took out a flashlight and swung its beam across the walls.

"Is there something you're looking for?" Ngozi pressed.

Yekini ignored him and turned to Tuoyo: "Did you scan the airlock before or after the repairs?"

"Both. Sweeps are automatic sequences within the pressurization and depressurization cycles."

Yekini pressed a button on the flashlight, and another light came on—ultraviolet. "Including a UV sweep?"

"No." Tuoyo frowned. "That's not included. Why would we want to do that?"

Yekini pulled out a medium-sized can and sprayed it in a spot. "To check for things that say that something alive was in here, perhaps?"

"Alive? You mean, like, my tech staff?"

"What's that?" asked Ngozi, pointing to her can.

"Luminol," said Yekini, spraying another spot. "And no, not your techs, who I'm sure were suited the whole time. I'm more concerned about anything else that was *not* them." She sprayed again. "Any fluid will show under luminol and UV— blood, semen, saliva, urine, sweat. For aquatics, we're looking for trimethylamine. That's what gives that fishy odor you're smelling."

Tuoyo knew that word—*trimethylamine*. After what happened with Nehikhare, she had done a lot of reading about the sinking of the *Centurion*—most of which she wasn't really supposed to have been doing. It was where she had come across this word.

Yekini was still spraying. "I'm just looking for traces. See if maybe something got in here that was big enough to—"

Yekini stopped short at a spot near the weld. She sprayed again, tentative. Reflexively, her hand reached for her firearm and paused there.

"What is it?" Ngozi asked.

Yekini gulped. Slowly, she sprayed from her can, in long, large bursts, over the welded panel. Then she clicked her UV light on and pointed it there.

It took a second, but slowly, the outlines came into view: sets of five digits, scattered all over the formerly split seam.

Fingers, maybe; toes, maybe. But the most prominent thing was that which connected them—the light membranes of a web.

"Children," Tuoyo whispered, and overhead, her dark cloud rumbled.

THE HAND THAT FEEDS IS SOMETIMES BITTEN

Dearest All-Infinite—

Remember when we
stretched forth arms and
breathed words and
the words gave
appetite?

Remember when we
brought forth wonders and
they called us gods and
we drank of
worship?

Remember when we
opened lips and
whispered stories that
they may live, that
they may have
vigor?

Who can stop the lion from hunting
    the antelope?
Can the grass wish the elephant does not
    flatten it?

Quickly you forget the nature of flesh;
not skin and bones but

wishes and tales.
Now witness flesh carve itself
over, over, into
nothingness.

Can tiger and opossum be
    siblings?

To conquer, is it not animal
    nature?

COMMISSION FOR THE PROTECTION OF THE FINGERS (COPOF)

HAZARD INTELLIGENCE REPORT

Note: This report is not finally evaluated intelligence.

File Metadata
Class: SECRET, TOP
Tower: PINNACLE
Subject: DEBRIEF: NTD SIGHTING #014, CLASS UPH
Date: DAY 172, YEAR 023

Summary: The following report is a detailed account of the sighting of a non-tower dweller (NTD) during a scientific expedition by the now-destroyed exploratory vessel, the *Centurion*. This report focuses specifically on physical descriptions of NTD014—colloquially referred to by surviving crew members as "mami wata." Intelligence gathered through interviews with surviving crew members has led us to label this NTD as unclassified (U) and potentially hostile (PH).

Report by: Mutiu Oladipo, Rank IV Analyst

Audio Transcript, Part I.

OLADIPO: Your name and designation for the record, sir.

ALIKA: Bos'n Eugene Alika, boatswain's mate of the watch.

O: Bos'n Alika, could you kindly describe, for the record, the events of Day 164, Year 023?

A: Okay. Uhm, I was sailing with my crew on the *Centurion,* with some researchers on board. Scientific exploration, typical OPL-assigned outing. We were doing the usual circle-around-the-tower reconnaissance mixed with a, uh, what's the word—

O: Anthropological survey?

A: Exactly. The scientists were supposed to look for connections to adapted life outside of the tower, and such.

O: When did you notice something was wrong?

A: The OOD—that's officer of the deck—said I should assign lookout shifts, and I did. But the lookout that was supposed to take his shift went missing.

O: Missing?

A: Yes. The lookout station is about three stories above deck. I radioed the station for a status update and did not hear anything back, so I went on deck and looked. Empty.

O: And what did you do?

A: Screamed *officer overboard,* of course! Extreme actions first is OPL Navy policy. I didn't want to assume he had simply abandoned his duty post.

O: And he hadn't?

A: No. His body still hasn't been found to this day.

O: Tell us what you did next.

A: I went up to the station to scout and spot him, in case he was still on the surface, while the crew lowered a lifeboat.

O: Was he? At surface, I mean.

A: Yes. Saw him with my two eyes. Right before . . . *something* dragged him under.

O: Dragged, you said?

A: Yes. Something with . . . *scales.*

O: Scales.

A: Yes. And then I was screaming at the lifeboat people to *turn around!* But they were too far to hear me.

O: What happened next?

A: The mami wata—

O: We're not calling it that right now, Bos'n Alika. We're going with non-tower dweller, unclassified and potentially hostile—NTD-UPH.

A: Well, NTD or whatever—call it what you want—but that *thing* came to surface and—and . . .

O: And?

A: *[unintelligible]* So many. So . . . *many.*

O: What did they do?

A: Tore the lifeboat to pieces.

O: Using what?

A: Teeth? I don't know! I was too far away. I just knew that they were not . . . human? In some parts, I think—I don't know. The first one I saw—I initially thought it was, like, a massive fish—a shark or something. But our aquatic ecosystem reports never mention such large sea life this close to the tower. Then I looked closer and realized it was not a fish—at least, not completely.

O: Describe what you saw as best as you can.

A: Let's see, ehm, I remember seeing a weed, almost like seaweed, you know? Right before its head came out of the water. Like a plant was growing on its spine. I remember sand—white, clean, like maybe if you put your foot at the bottom of the ocean and pull it out. Fish eyes. Scales, smooth and shiny. Like a frog mixed with fish mixed with us, you know? I don't know if what I'm saying makes sense . . .

O: It just has to be honest.

A: Can I swear in the Savior's name? I swear to it. They were just . . . there are no words to describe it. And then its eyes. Those fish eyes were—I don't know if red and glowing was my imagination, but it looked like that, especially after they tore the lifeboat to shreds.

O: And then?

A: Then one of them turned, and it looked at our ship. And deep in those
   eyes, it's like I saw . . .

O: What, Bos'n Alika? What did you see?

A: Hate. All I saw was hate.

End of "Audio Transcript, Part I."

*Addendum: Upon multiple consultations with the master clerics,
NTD014-UPH is now collectively referred to in contemporary usage as
"Children of Yemoja."*

YEKINI

Yekini, exiting the airlock dazed. Tuoyo, equally disoriented, maintaining just enough presence of mind to lock down the chamber and bar unauthorized entry. Ngozi, for the first time looking like someone had frozen him in ice, his silence a breath of fresh air. All three shambling, a trio of zombies making their way back to the foreman's workroom.

What are the chances? Yekini thought. *On my first field assignment!* How could this be anything but a curse? She tried to imagine it: coming face-to-face with one of *Yemoja's Children*—their full designation according to the OPL (since they were, in the words of the master clerics, *offspring of the devils beneath the sea*). She couldn't decide if she'd be afraid or amazed.

If anyone was completely flattened by this, though, it was Tuoyo. As they wound through a maze of corridors on the way to her office, some of her colleagues offered pleasantries but she did not answer. Almost every single colleague, upon seeing her accompanied by two officials dressed in the manner they were—and judging by one look at them, midders—stopped. They asked her what was wrong, if she was okay, if she needed any help, if she needed them to tag along for her sake. She answered with a robotic, repetitive, jerky "I'm fine" and resumed her glazed-eye forward gaze.

It wasn't until minutes later that Yekini realized they had gone past this same place before. The woman had lost track of her bearings.

Yekini stepped forward and put a hand on Tuoyo's shoulder. "Maybe you should stop and reorient before we continue."

"Hmm?"

"You're taking us in circles."

Tuoyo looked around, like she was just waking from a dream. "Oh."

"Here, give me your handheld," Yekini said, taking the device from the woman. "I'll find the directions myself. What's your workroom number?"

Yekini located the map and directions, led them back to Tuoyo's tiny workroom, and had the woman sit down. She found her a bag to breathe into. Ngozi went outside to pace, as the tiny room could barely fit all three of them.

Yekini looked about the place. It lay in slight disarray the way only an engineer's office could: a collection of safety equipment hung on a wall (earmuffs, gloves, kneepads); a half-uncoupled device in the corner that looked like it was for ancient communications (so many *wires*); a half-eaten meat roll on the table. Most of the furniture was shabby and worn, yet at the same time, had a cleanliness about it, in the way of someone who once cared about appearance and was now slowly forgetting how to.

It was one of the vestiges of Midder life, that focus on neatness. Yekini knew this firsthand—every now and then, she would come into the office after lunch with a stain on her clothing and receive deathly stares. Once, she had been queried and even had a one-on-one with Director Merit just because the woman thought she wasn't *presentable enough*.

This was how she understood what must've happened to Tuoyo. Her partner must've been the midder of them both, and must've elevated her to midder status as well. And since Midder living was so regulated, so mechanical and controlled, it wouldn't have taken long for it to become ingrained in Tuoyo. Then when her partner had died, of course she'd have been asked to go back down to wherever the hell she came from. She would have been forced to lose her midder self all over again.

"What do we do now?" Tuoyo asked.

"I'm thinking," Yekini said. "We obviously need to report it at some point, but my first worry is: Do we do so *now,* or wait until we have clear and absolute proof? Upstairs won't take it kindly if we come rushing in without conclusive evidence. We've already sent in two inconclusive reports today."

Tuoyo nodded. "So we . . . wait?"

"Investigate further, yes," Yekini said. "If that . . . if *it* has found its way into this tower . . ." She trailed off. "Was there video surveillance in that chamber?"

"In an airlock?" For a moment, Tuoyo seemed to think it a joke, but when she saw Yekini's serious expression, comported herself. "No."

"And outside?"

"I've looked at the feeds. Hours and hours. Nothing. One moment the sluice gate was there, another moment, broken."

"And you didn't see the moment *when* it broke?"

"It's underwater," said Tuoyo. "Things are always moving, and what we get is shifting images, not really real time."

Yekini puffed her cheeks and blew. "Okay, okay. Let's start here: You have a plan of this level?"

Tuoyo turned on her station while Yekini went outside to meet Ngozi. He stood directly under a light source (the hallway was poorly lit), tapping furiously at his wearable and attracting attention from passersby. Especially as he had somehow taken off the gear she'd given him and was now back in his suit that screamed *government official,* which was pretty much the same thing as *enemy* down here. The stares weren't friendly, but he obviously did not notice, and even if he did, Yekini guessed he wouldn't care.

"This stupid thing—" He tapped at it again. "This stupid *place.* I cannot connect to the server and send my report from all the way down here because of limited range. Someone should've told me we'd be so far down I'd have no access, but no, *someone* left out that piece of vital information."

"Are you always blaming people for your problems?" Before he answered, Yekini put up a hand. "Never mind. Why are you calling upstairs?"

"Why am I—" He snorted. "To report the situation, of course."

"I don't think we should do that just yet," Yekini said. "Perhaps wait until we have more evidence?"

"*More* evidence?" Ngozi said. "We need more evidence than *that*?"

"Hands and feet tell us nothing."

"Name *one* thing you know that has webbed hands and feet."

"We don't have *conclusive* evidence," Yekini stressed. "Those were imprints. Anyone could've put those there. We should file a report when we have stronger evidence, like, I don't know, clear and obvious video?"

"There were cameras in there?"

"No. But the foreman is pulling up the layout of all tunnels on this level. I'm trying to see the extent of that airlock wall, what spaces it connects to. If there's a Child within these walls, it will have to exit somewhere, and if that *somewhere* has a camera—boom, video evidence."

This seemed rational enough to calm him down. "Fine," he said, turning off the wearable. "Fine."

They went back in the workroom. Tuoyo had shrugged off her flustered demeanor and was frowning over her handheld.

"What is it?" Ngozi asked.

"I think our non-tower dweller has already found an exit."

All three crowded around the handheld. On it, there was a looping feed of an empty space—a small room or wide corridor. Nothing seemed amiss at first. But then, in the next frame, the seam on a nearby wall panel suddenly had an opening, just like what had happened in the airlock. The feed looped again, starting with the seam shut. In the next frame, it was open again. Shut, open, repeat.

Yekini peered at the time between. Bare seconds.

"This is how the outside feed was too," Tuoyo was saying. "Except, this is closer to real-time, so we should be seeing . . . *it* come out of there."

"Unless," Yekini said, surprised she was even entertaining this possibility, "we can't see them."

"Yes, that's what she said—"

"No, you're not listening to me," she said. "I think the Child *is* in that video. We just can't see it."

They turned their attention back to the loop, as the horror of it slowly dawned on them.

"Children are . . . *invisible*?" whispered Tuoyo.

"Oh, *come on*!" said Ngozi. "Invisible Children? You two must be smarter than this. We don't even know that Children exist!"

"They exist," said Tuoyo, quietly but firmly, in a way that even Ngozi knew not to dispute. He turned to Yekini instead.

"Madam Agent," he said. "You're the expert. Tell us—does COPOF intelligence say this about Children?"

As part of orientation into the COPOF, Yekini had received the standard novice agent trainings and briefings on the five security threat levels that, as the learning materials proclaimed, *threaten the continuous and harmonious existence of the Fingers*. The first two—*minimal* and *limited*—meant the threats were out of mind but not out of sight, so were mostly internal threats like dissenters and resistance groups who refused to adhere to the Pinnacle's regulations. *High-level* threats were those where words were actually put into action, like the few lowers who would decide, every now and then, to take their fight to the midders and uppers (it never ended well for them). *High-level* was also used for major criminal activities like armed robbery, which were rare, but still happened. *Imminent* was for threats from outside the Pinnacle, specifically created in the wake of the disturbances that had crumbled and sank the other towers.

Critical was for anything that came from undersea. The real ocean deep and the creatures it held was still too far out from here. At this range, there was only one source of critical danger: Yemoja's Children.

Unlike the other threat levels, the Children were not part of an agency briefing given to Yekini and her orientation group. To learn about Children, they had been taken to the Pinnacle's archtemple, the seat of spiritual worship in the tower. There, an elderly master cleric sat them down and told them the history of the devil spawn that was Yemoja's Children and what they were capable of.

Yekini never quite left there with a clear sense of who the Children were or what they were capable of. Every now and then, when the OPL dispersed security feeds about external threats, Yekini, like most people, left with a clear sense of the threat posed to Pinnacle dwellers, but not of why Yemoja's Children posed said threat. Some people thought of them as monster-ghosts who could slip through walls. Some thought of them as magma-spitting demons, complete with little horns tucked into their hair. Some thought of them as shape-shifting ancient warriors with sharklike teeth. The OPL did not discourage any of this thinking, and rather helped recycle and re-feed these images, especially through the archtemple and its subsidiaries' homilies.

The only thing everyone agreed upon was that they looked obviously humanlike and could pass for one. The trick was to check their hands and feet for webbing, and behind their ears for gills. Yekini found all of this odd: How could one check for such when everyone agreed that Children could not survive outside of water? Had anyone captured any of these creatures and presented them as evidence?

This was her sticking point, now, when this question came to the fore.

"I know only what you know," she said to Ngozi and Tuoyo. "I've never seen a Child with my own two eyes before, and I don't know what they can do. I suspect no one does. I'm not prone to believing things without evidence." She pointed at the handheld. "That, there, is evidence, and I'm happy to get behind it."

A notification light flashed on somewhere, bathing the room in orange. It came from Tuoyo's station. She jabbed at a button. "What?"

"Chief," a male voice said on the other end, almost breathless. "Chief . . ."

Tuoyo frowned. "Emeka? What?"

"Something here—" He cut off. "Something—" He cut off again, as if he were running, or speaking to someone at the same time, or both.

All three in the room glanced at one another, puzzled.

"Emeka?" Tuoyo called. "Are you there?"

The voice came back. "Yes." He gulped, audibly. "Chief, you need to come down here oh. North end, close to Refrigeration. Blood everywhere."

YEKINI

Good news: nobody was dead. Bad news: there *was* blood everywhere.

A small trail, initially. But someone had—likely in error—slipped in it, carving a ghastly, slick shape on the floor. Red bootprints littered the hallway. Someone, perhaps morbidly fascinated by blood, had also handprinted the walls with it.

Then there was the person from whom the blood was oozing, sitting with his back to a wall, letting out intermittent moans of pain. Very much alive, but dazed, pale, scared to the bone. One side of his head continued to leak blood as he held a dirty, soaked rag to it.

Ngozi turned into a corner and retched.

The workman who'd called it in—Emeka, Tuoyo had called him—had done the unenviable job of clearing the scene of onlookers and securing it until help came. He'd solicited the aid of level vigilantes, three burly men in heavy belts and uniforms that looked hand-sewn, carrying batons. They blocked the entry and exit points to the area and redirected traffic.

Tuoyo, after standing and gazing into space for a bit, led Emeka to a corner and began to quiz him about what had happened and how he had discovered the blood. It was Yekini, then, who took charge and knelt by the man.

"Don't touch anything!" Ngozi tried not to turn around so he wouldn't see the blood. "Shouldn't we wait until police arrive?"

"They'll take years to come down here," Yekini said. Pinnacle Police barely left the Midders, so much so that many levels in the Lowers had to form their own vigilante crews to combat anyone driven to crime due to overcrowding, lack of resources, or deficient infrastructure. Whenever police actually ventured down here, it was more to harass dwellers than aid them in any useful way. Yekini didn't think they'd be particularly interested in chasing the lead down if they found out a Child might be involved. That was the job of COPOF agents like her.

"What happened?" Yekini asked the man softly. "What did you see?"

The man didn't acknowledge her presence, continuing to stare into space in shock. Yekini suspected a serious concussion, slamming and wounding his head like that. Trying to eke information out of him would be futile.

She felt for his pulse—weak. She searched his pockets. Nothing unusual. She unlocked his wearable and used hers to scan the biochip in his forearm, retrieving his information. A base-level workman who worked in the Refrigeration unit. Nothing particularly noteworthy.

She tapped at his wearable to see his last few actions. He'd tried to ping the emergency line minutes before. She rose and looked around, and for the first time, realized why he was in this specific position. An emergency button hung on the wall a few feet away. Blood had splattered over it in such a way that it was no longer visible.

He did not just trip and fall. He'd been running *away* from something.

And either that thing had attacked him as he'd been trying to alert everybody, or it had caused him to injure himself.

She went back and guided Tuoyo and Ngozi into a corner.

"You're not going to like this," she said.

"More than all this blood?" Ngozi asked.

"I think he was attacked by . . ." Yekini took a deep breath. It sounded ridiculous, trying to get it out of her mouth—*How could something no one had testified to seeing be guilty of an attack?* "I think there was a Child here."

Tuoyo exhaled audibly. "If that's the case . . . are we saying it's already in the hallways? In the tower, with us?"

With us. Yekini fought down a shiver.

"I don't know. But we need to find a way to be a hundred percent sure so we can act fast. If we spend time chasing the wrong thing and end up with more attacks, we'll have even more trouble on our hands."

"So what are you saying?" asked Ngozi.

"We need to clear this level. Right now."

"We don't have the authorization to do that." Ngozi tut-tutted. "See, this is why I said we should've reported back immediately."

"Wouldn't have changed anything. This happened too quickly after our discovery anyway."

"Ehn, but we're still standing here. Me, I'm done listening to you people." Ngozi turned around and started off. "Madam Foreman, I'm going to ping my office from your station, and then I'm getting out of this cursed place. I can't be trapped down here if this nonsense escalates."

When he was out of earshot, Tuoyo motioned to Yekini.

"He's an idiot but he may be right. This is as far as we can go without reporting. If this level needs clearing and lockdown, we'll need authorization, and we'll need it fast."

"Have you thought about where everyone will go?" Yekini asked. Tuoyo shook her head. "Because now that I think of it, level ten above or level eight below are not going to just welcome everyone with open arms. A few refugees, yes, they'll take, but a *whole* level, all four wings? That's *a lot* of people."

Tuoyo shrugged. "That sounds like an OPL problem. Our job is just to make recommendations, right?" She turned to where Emeka stood whispering to one of the level vigilantes and said to him: "Ping me when the police arrive?"

YEKINI

Back in the tiny workroom, Ngozi was already seated at the station and had placed a call through to his office. He occupied Tuoyo's chair, a move Yekini considered distasteful, while Tuoyo slumped into another in the corner, too preoccupied with having seen one of her people wounded. Yekini sat opposite Ngozi, in the visitor's chair, and waited.

The screen came alive. A secretary sat in front of a sigil that said OFFICE OF THE PINNACLE LEADERSHIP. At its center was an outline of the five Fingers—still carrying the ancient, now-defunct name, the DIEKARA ATLANTIC COMMUNITY—with the Pinnacle highlighted.

"Direct transfer for Deputy Director Azubuike, please," Ngozi said. Before the man behind the desk could get another word out, Ngozi said, "Tell him it's from Nwafor—ID number four-zero-four-seven-two-nine—and it's critical. Remember to say *critical*."

The secretary nodded and the screen went into a hold video for a moment, the music and narration of which promptly filled the room.

The video was a variation of the same promotion the OPL liked to keep on repeat, to keep in front of people's minds. It was the same three-step sequence each time. First, a reminder of how the Fingers saved them from the flood and from the world that Old Lagos had belonged to. Yekini noted that this particular hold video did not show the beautiful sides of Old Lagos she saw in a few of the archival images she had access to as a COPOF agent, but rather displayed footage of the ugliest of what had once existed: crowded marketplaces, rickety vehicles in haphazard parks, all the telltale signs of squalor. Almost as if this message was tailored to the lowers, as if they weren't allowed to fathom what progress and luxury looked like.

Next, a statement that lauded the "Great Atlantic Fingers" for coming to the rescue, and for all its achievements, and then enjoined everyone to follow the precepts of the tower if they were to prevent a return to the days of the destroyed. This employed the same stock footage Yekini was used to: of the arch-temple and its master clerics, dressed in their lengthy, flowing immaculate-white robes; of orderly, sharply dressed people in plain colors, referred to as "the good citizens of the tower," or colloquially, "the best towerzens"; and lastly, of the Pinnacle prime, the man whose forerunners designed the towers and made the Fingers happen, who remained at the very top and never came down—Amos Diekara himself.

It was the prime who ushered in the third sequence, the one where, in his never-changing ensemble of gray-brown T-shirt beneath a gray-brown blazer, crow's-feet eyes and full gray beard beneath graying hair, he went on to explain why it was important to keep these rules, why it was important to ensure that the enemies who sought to destroy the towers were never allowed to gain foothold. He casually offered a compendium of said enemies: "those from within who look, talk and act like you, who may even be your family members, but hold spirits of hostility and disharmony in their hearts," and "those from without, devilish abominations the sea has brought forth from the depths of debauchery that was the old nations." Then, in the final shot, he was joined by the master clerics and good towerzens from the earlier sequence, and there they all stood at the very top, enjoying the benefits of Pinnacle living.

Of course, Yekini knew it was all edited footage. No one had ever seen the top of the Pinnacle, not even police or the master clerics, two groups among the few that were allowed movement between levels. Yekini wondered if even the image of the prime himself was projected. No towerzen she knew had ever stood next to the prime and returned. It was assumed that if anyone ever went up and set their naked eyes on the prime, there was no way they were coming back down.

The video looped a few more times before a grim-faced man

appeared on the screen, seated behind a large desk. The screen titled him as KELECHI AZUBUIKE: DEPUTY DIRECTOR, OFFICE OF THE PINNACLE LEADERSHIP. He was squeezed into a chair that would've complained if it could, and looked like someone who was always angry—which made sense, seeing as he was the highest-ranked public-facing official in Pinnacle leadership. Every other facet of Pinnacle leadership did not interact with the towerzens. He alone was scapegoat and screen.

"Good morning, sir," Ngozi hailed enthusiastically. "It's Nwafor."

The man's expression shifted only slightly. "Ngozi," he said, using his first name. "Kedụ?"

"Ọ di mma." Ngozi beamed. Yekini frowned. It was against tower regulations to use languages from the old nation in public dealings, but she wasn't surprised. Lots of people had remained defiant and found ways to pass their languages down to their offspring—and once a language was known, people were bound to speak it. That these two were government officials supposed to be holding up these laws meant little. Yekini's own Maame had even once tried to teach her the old Yoruba and Arabic. Yekini didn't get far with either.

Azubuike leaned into the screen, peering. "Ke bi nọ?"

"I'm in the Lowers, sir," Ngozi said.

"The *Lowers*?" Azubuike's eyes narrowed. "Doing what there? Who sent you a message?"

"I got assigned this morning oh," Ngozi said. "They said to check out a breach."

"Breach of what?"

"A floodable airlock. Something about a broken sluice gate and an open wall seam." The words flowed from Ngozi's lips like he was some kind of expert. Yekini hated that he was benefiting so much from someone else's expertise. Scumbag.

"Why am I just hearing this?" Azubuike leaned away from the screen and shouted a name, then returned. "I didn't know. I would never have allowed them to send one of my top-performing staff down to the gutters."

Ngozi cleared his throat and glanced at the two women to see if they noticed. Yekini made a mock performance of rolling her eyes.

"Eh yes, well, it was supposed to be a routine check, sir."

"I see." Azubuike went back to working, speaking without looking up. "Why are you disturbing me with a routine check, then? Please carry yourself back up here immediately."

"Sir, did your secretary not tell you? It's no longer routine. It's now critical."

"Critical how?"

"We believe at least one Child has entered the tower and attacked a workman."

Azubuike's fingers stopped flying across the lit keyboard. He slowly glanced up.

"*You said what?*"

"We believe we have found evidence of a Child in the tower, sir."

"Who is *we*?"

"I'm here with the level nine foreman and a COPOF agent—an analyst, really. They sent her down here to take a look. She's the one who discovered the Child's presence."

"Analyst," Azubuike said, and Yekini realized he was asking for her. She went around the desk and leaned into the frame.

"Sir."

"What's this I'm hearing?"

"Mr. Nwafor is correct. We found a trail of something that has clearly come from undersea, and it's definitely not us—not tower citizens—sir."

"And someone is *dead*?"

"No, injured. A workman on this level, but we have no clear indications as to what happened. We only assume he was attacked or fleeing from . . . something, judging by the nature of his injuries."

"And you think this *something* is . . . a Child?"

"We're working with that theory, yes."

"Savior above! And you *waited* all this time to tell me?"

Azubuike was speaking to Ngozi now, but quickly returned to Yekini. "And you—have you made a report of this to your superior?"

"No, sir," Yekini said. "We were waiting—"

Azubuike cut her off before she could breathe. He remained on-screen but had them muted. They could see him suddenly agitated, moving around—even Tuoyo rose and came to watch the scene with some interest. After a moment of him fussing about with an off-screen thing or two, he rose and left, leaving them with a spinning chair.

"Well, this is just wonderful," Ngozi said, and leaned back. "If I get queried for this, just know I'll ensure I'm not the only one."

"Oh, shut up already," Yekini said. "*Query* this, *superior* that. Somebody almost *died* on this level, and all you have are threats and concerns about stupid promotions."

Ngozi was aghast. "Who do you think you're talking to?"

"Just shut up," Yekini spat back. "File a report about my behavior when you return, for all I care, but while you're here *shut. the. fuck. up*."

Before Ngozi could offer a rebuttal, the screen came back alive.

It was no longer one view, but a split view. On the new side of the screen was Yekini's boss, Merit Timipre, director of CO-POF. The woman, in her sharp suit and contacts that made her eyes look gray and dead, gazed down with a sour expression that told Yekini she was definitely in for it when she went back up to level 66.

"Agent Yekini, Mr. Nwafor, Engineer Odili," Director Merit said, her flinty tone bringing them to attention in a way Yekini was familiar with, but the others weren't, evident in the way they perked up—almost startled. "You are being rerouted to a secure channel. Please hold for transfer. In the meantime, I'd like you to lock the door of whatever unit you're in, if you don't mind."

This time, a video did not play during the hold. Instead, they sat watching the two officials, while Tuoyo locked the door and returned. Yekini had never been on a secure channel before, but she knew what this meant. They were about to speak to someone important, someone who was not in the public eye like the two people they were speaking to currently. Someone behind the screen.

"May I ask who we're meeting, Director?" she ventured.

Merit did not respond, which did not matter because there was a ping a moment after, and a third screen appeared to join the other two.

"You are now speaking directly to the Pinnacle prime," Merit said, "Proceed with discretion."

Then the two directors hung up, and the three were left alone in the workroom with the man at the top of the world.

OFFICE OF THE PINNACLE LEADERSHIP

Entry #R-1103
Start of excerpt.

THE PAN-AFRICAN INTERNATIONALIST

Rising Tides, Lowering Hopes: West Africa's Cities Battle Coastal Erosion

Relocating residents from West Africa's coastal areas has opened up a can of worms: land grabs, state-enforced evictions, and capitalist-driven, climate-based excuses for gentrification. **Vienna Black** *reports.*

18 October 2031

Longtime residents of the Nigerian megalopolis of Lagos are no strangers to the ferocity of water. The city's proximity to the Atlantic Ocean and its low-lying topography have long left it vulnerable to coastal erosion. As changes to the environment rage on—for worse—the city faces threats of new levels of devastation, and the poorest of inhabitants—those least responsible for these environmental changes—are at the mercy of it all.

About two in three Lagosians live in slums, and a significant number of these communities reside dangerously within reach of the shore. Scientists and socioeconomic experts studying these phenomena have advised the governments of Lagos and Nigeria—and other similar provincial and national governments on the continent's western edge—to stage a managed retreat of these at-risk communities if they are to be protected from the threat posed by rising seas.

Instead, the Lagos state governor has, under the guise of environmental protection, issued a flurry of eviction notices to shoreside slum communities, a practice developed during the colonial era between the mid-nineteenth century and 1960, sharpened with the violent Otodo Gbame eviction of 2016—which resulted in 30,000 people being displaced—and repeatedly employed since then. Often, the lands seized in these grabs are then offered to capitalist ventures and investors who gentrify them for more economic purposes from which the government benefits.

"Governments and policymakers have chosen to focus their strategic plans on securing economic structures," says Emmanuel Akindayo, who hails from Lagos and is a professor of geography and environmental management at the University of Waterloo. "Businesses and infrastructure—most of which do not benefit these vulnerable populations, mind you—are at the forefront of their salvage attempts. Look at Diekara Industries and their plans for their towers, for instance. Look at their barges out there, digging and digging into sand that used to safeguard poor communities and fun beaches before the water overran it all. The government pocketed millions and cleared everything out of the way just for these vampires to build their fancy island. Imagine the inhumanity of that."

End of excerpt.

YEKINI

Yekini had never thought of Pinnacle Prime Citizen Amos Diekara as anything more than the man at the top in the gray-brown suit—an image, a persona. But staring directly at him now, for the first time, even though through a screen, she was suddenly taken aback by how much of a *person* he was. Maybe it was the fact that he was dressed in something different: a casual shirt of bright green that brought focus to his face. He suddenly looked younger, sprightly, even though his full gray beard said otherwise. The wrinkles under his eyes were not those of old age (he was only in his fifties) or stress from working too hard (Yekini presumed the prime worked the least of every towerzen), but wrinkles you got from worrying constantly about how to carry on the legacy of towers handed down from your father to you, and to him from his father before.

Maame was always telling Yekini of a christ man called Jesus and his eternal antagonist, someone or something called the *anti-christ*. Whenever Yekini thought of what this anti-christ might look like, she envisioned this man.

Amos Diekara wore the disposition of someone who had been enjoying something else before being interrupted by this call. More bored than irritated, perhaps because he was speaking to three underlings whom he wouldn't have touched with a pole on a regular day.

The three underlings, on the other hand, shrank into themselves, unable to open their mouths, or in the case of Tuoyo, close it now that it was already open. Ngozi looked starstruck in a way that told Yekini that his goal in life might actually be to *become* prime, which was ridiculous because only Diekaras became primes. Yekini found herself, yet again, the only one to recover composure.

"Your Excellency," she said, and bowed her head slightly,

unsure of what the requisite greeting for this situation was. The others saw her and followed suit.

"Hmm," Amos Diekara said, neither correcting nor assenting to her address. He drank from a nearby glass, peering into the screen. "I can't . . ." He leaned forward, squinting. "Why is it so dark there? I can barely see your faces."

"I—uhm—well." Tuoyo seemed horrified. "That is all the light we have here, sir."

"Really?" For a moment, he looked genuinely concerned. "That's not right. We should do something about that."

The three glanced at one another. Was that a thing that could even happen?

"Now, what's this business about a Child in the tower?" He said this noncommittally, like Children in the tower happened every day. "I hear someone's dead."

"No, sir," Ngozi said, taking over before Yekini could get a word in. "*Injured*. We believe at least one Child has broken into level nine of the tower and wounded one of the workmen."

"How did it get in?"

"We found a breach in a floodable airlock, sir," Ngozi said. "We think it might've moved through the walls."

"The *walls*?"

"Yes, sir. There are . . . spaces."

"Huh." This seemed to be news to him. Yekini wondered how this man knew so little about his own tower.

"You have no idea where it might be now?"

"No, Your Excellency," Ngozi replied.

"So, it could be running about the tower, wreaking havoc as we speak, is that so?"

Ngozi looked at the two women in supplication. Yekini gave him a look of *Oh now you want to look at me, Mr. I'm-In-Charge*.

"That's not good." Diekara said this as if it were a question, as if he wanted them to answer.

"I don't believe it is, sir," Ngozi said quietly.

"More horrible things could come of this if we let it go on for too long."

"Yes, sir."

"Hmm." He drank again. "Well, thank you for being prompt in your delivery of this critical information. You are more prime towerzen than myself, and the Pinnacle would like to thank you for your service to its safety and future."

"Thank you, sir." Ngozi beamed like a child offered sweets.

"Sir, if I may," Yekini dropped in, to Ngozi's alarm.

"Yes?" Diekara squinted again. "And you are?"

"Agent Yekini Yekini, COPOF."

"Which one is that one again?"

"Commission for the Protection of the Fingers."

"Ah, yes. Right, carry on, what is it?"

"I think we may need to evacuate this level as soon as possible. I believe that's the easiest way to prevent any more harm to tower citizens. I believe this is something that might require your express approval, sir."

"Wait, hold on now." Diekara's interest was suddenly sparked. "That's quite drastic. I understand what you're saying, but we should leave evacuation as a final course of action."

"But sir," Yekini pressed, to Ngozi's growing indignation, "perhaps that might be too late? We waited only less than an hour, and there is already one wounded person."

"*Agent,*" Diekara said, firmer now, sounding like the prime that he was. "Do you know the resources an evacuation requires? Do you know what people have to undergo during a level evacuation?"

Yekini balked. "No, sir."

"An evacuation means moving the citizens of one level to another, which not only doubles the population of that new level, but also means you have people from two different levels coexisting. That's not ideal. Imagine if everyone from level eight was suddenly dumped on you there in level nine? Or the level ten-ers were suddenly told to pack their bags and move to your level. Just imagine it. The overcrowding, the infighting, the scarcity. That kind of imbalance is completely against the ideology of this tower. In our history, large movements of people such as in an evacuation have only ever been a last recourse, and only when the levels in question are equipped to handle them." He sipped from his glass. "We wait and seek other courses of action first."

Yekini did not have an answer to that lengthy brush-off, so she kept her mouth shut. Ngozi, who now had a permanent frown plastered on his forehead, turned back to the screen.

"Sir, we will await further instructions from our bosses."

"That is right," Diekara said. He was back to bored. "I will rendezvous with my security board, and you will hear from us soon. Sit tight."

"Thank you, Your Excellency," Ngozi said.

"And thank you, Mr. . . . what's your name?"

"Ngozi Nwafor, sir, category one administrator from your office, sir."

"My office?"

"The Office of the Pinnacle Leadership, sir."

"Ah, right, yes. That's good. Maybe when you come back up, I'd like to thank you in person."

"Sir!" Ngozi saluted awkwardly. "That would be the best day of my life!"

"Yes, right." Diekara looked back to Yekini. "And thank you too, Agent Yekini. And . . ." He peered again. "I believe I was told you were three?"

Yekini looked at Tuoyo, who had been standing there all this time, quiet. She saw something in the woman's eyes—it wasn't hate, but it was something close, like this man had personally offended her. To be honest, Yekini had come away with the vibe that Tuoyo thought of everything she didn't want around her as an irritation, but this was different. This looked like she had a personal vendetta.

"Tuoyo Igudia, level nine foreman," she said, and it was cold, and maybe a little sad. Yekini frowned at her use of a different last name, but said nothing of it.

"Right. Thank you all, and now await further instructions." Diekara went off as quickly as he'd come, and the feed died.

"How can you be so annoying so many times in one day?" Ngozi launched, turning on Yekini. "So much so that you even annoyed the prime!"

"Fuck off," Yekini said, then turned to Tuoyo, who had shrunk back into the darkness, facing the wall in the corner of the room. "Tuoyo, what's up? What's the problem?"

"Oh wow, me *fuck off,* okay." Ngozi went to the opposite corner. Yekini followed Tuoyo as she sank into a chair.

"Are you okay?" Yekini asked softly, a hand on her shoulder.

"He doesn't even know." Tuoyo's voice was lifeless, stripped of affect.

"Sorry?"

"She gave her life for this tower," she said, "and he doesn't even know her name."

NGOZI

The wait had now stretched out to a couple of hours, yet there were still no updates. Ngozi found it difficult to concentrate. He needed, more than anything, to get out of this place and back to sanity. He had never cherished his boring life until this moment, when its comforts were levels away from reach.

Yekini and Tuoyo had gone off to deal with the police's arrival, leaving him alone in the workroom. He sat in the darkness, hoping that all of this would turn out fine, soon filed away into *let's-never-discuss-that* land. The level 9 worker would get treatment, the women would be queried, and he'd hopefully get rewarded for his levelheadedness during this period of distress. He'd gained proximity to the prime—that about ensured it.

He slipped a hand into his shirt and fiddled with the pendant of his orange-peel necklace.

"We did it, sis," he whispered to the empty unit. "We dreamed, we stayed alive, and now we're rising. I've just spoken directly to a Diekara! We have *access* now, sis!"

He tucked the necklace back. He had done the work, but it was yet unfinished. If the women were right about the Child, for instance, then everyone on this level—himself included—was in danger. He couldn't fulfill his duty or honor every sacrifice if he died while out on a simple rotten assignment.

The two women returned, ejecting him from his musing.

"They called yet?" Yekini asked.

"No."

She frowned. "What's wrong with you?"

"Nothing."

"I think that's just how his face is," Tuoyo said, and the two women snickered. How could they even be *laughing* at a time like this?

"You've just come back from the scene of a bloody attack,"

he said slowly, surprising even himself with the placidity in his voice, "yet you're gallivanting in here, trying to be funny."

"Okay, wow, you're an intense man," Yekini said with exaggeration.

Tuoyo snickered again. Ngozi didn't think it was *that* clever, throwing his words back at him. But he'd walked right into it, so perhaps that was a little deserved.

"Police have dispersed personnel to search every corner of this level." Yekini was back to a serious tone. "They're working hand in hand with upstairs, so they should deal with the situation soon enough. Or so we hope. Either way, it's out of our hands now."

True to word, an announcement went out right then over the system. Everyone was to stay indoors in any units available to them, while police searched the level. No one was allowed to leave the level until the search had been duly completed.

Wonderful, thought Ngozi. *More time in the underworld cavern.*

Minutes later, there was a knock on their workroom door, and someone shouted, "Police!"

They opened for a man and a woman to enter, dressed in red-and-white uniforms and heavy kits—vests, firearms, flashlights, grip boots: almost like Yekini herself, if not for their berets that proudly screamed *Pinnacle Police Force.* They peered into every corner of the workroom while the three waited outside. The man opened the office cooler and made a sound at the amount of half-eaten food in there. The woman shined a flashlight in places that made Tuoyo wince. All in all, they were out and on to the next unit in a jiffy.

Yekini kissed her teeth as they left. "Did they expect to find a Child in your cooler? Wasting all this time when an evacuation would've been safer and less time-consuming."

"And take the easy way when they can just bully us instead?" Tuoyo wrinkled her nose. "You give them too much credit."

They returned to the unit and waited.

"No one is safe until whatever made those prints is found," said Yekini. "Child or not, I don't care—but that question must be answered."

"They did make a good point about how the Child—if it's one—could follow us to another level if we had an evacuation," said Tuoyo. "Not that I'm against Children going up, though. If anything, I'm happy for them to crawl up there and eat every upper's brain or something."

"Won't they go past the Midders first?" Ngozi asked, pointing to himself and Yekini. "We are midders."

"Then they can eat your brain too," said Tuoyo before pointing to Yekini. "Not you, though. I like you."

Yekini laughed. "See, even if Children could live outside of water, they still can't breach the Uppers. Only someone with a death wish would try to go past all the defense systems in the Midder-Upper transition."

"Or maybe upstairs will just shut themselves off and leave us to the mercy of the Children," said Tuoyo. "They don't care a lick about us anyway."

"You keep saying *them*," Ngozi said.

The women looked at him.

"Aren't you both one of *them*? Don't you work, directly or indirectly, for the OPL?"

"Eh," said Tuoyo. "Fuck the uppers."

But Yekini looked more like the question had sparked something in her. She shrugged, and Ngozi could see her confidence falter, indecision dancing in the light behind her eyes.

"I've only ever wanted to *protect*," she said broodingly. "I joined the COPOF because I wanted to help the people of this tower live their best lives without worrying about their safety. I didn't want to work for the OPL, and in many ways, I still don't. Advocating for the well-being of every towerzen is what drives me, and always will. Right now, that's what I'm advocating for when I say everyone on this level should be evacuated."

The room was quiet after that, each of them ruminating.

Ngozi, for a brief moment, attempted to consider what his own foremost desire was born of, and why he should even care, when suddenly a long, hard emergency blast punctured the still air.

"What in the Savior's name . . . ?" Yekini shot to her feet and opened the door.

Outside, the hallways had turned red, emergency lights overtaking everything. The floor had suddenly lit up with directions. People were milling out of their units, confused, most heading over to where Yekini stood outside the door with Tuoyo and Ngozi.

Not a single police officer in sight.

Tuoyo pulled her handheld from the office and poked at it. "Ehm, people, *people!*" She looked stricken. "We need to follow those lights and get off this level, immediately!"

"What—why?" Ngozi snatched the handheld from her, but couldn't understand what he was seeing, except that one corner of what was shaped like the tower itself—*Overhead plan of the level,* he realized quickly—was blinking, and the controls by its side said: SLUICE GATE OPEN.

"Is that—" He peered closer. "Is that the *airlock*?"

"Yes." She looked ashen. "Someone just opened the sluice gates."

"Why?" Yekini asked.

"I don't know—I didn't do it. But that airlock is now flooding *fast.*"

"Then *undo* it."

"I—" Tuoyo tapped furiously at the handheld. "I no longer have access!"

The emergency alarms intensified, the noise bouncing off all the level's metal surfaces and ricocheting into something forceful, angry.

"Where are all the police?" Yekini said suddenly. Ngozi looked about. Not a single one in sight.

"Oh no," Tuoyo said again, peering into her handheld.

"What now?" Yekini inched closer, as did more workers, some starting to whisper questions.

"The airlock," Tuoyo said. "I locked it with my personal code."

"So?"

"So?" She looked up, aghast. "Whoever opened the sluice gates is now trying to *open* the door!"

"*Open* it?" Ngozi's eyes widened. "The whole level will flood!"

The weight of that revelation fell on them in a wave of silence, like an angel passing.

"That's why the police are suddenly missing," Yekini said slowly. She turned to Ngozi and Tuoyo, to all the workers gathered around, looked them in the eye, and uttered the words her comrades were too afraid to say:

"The OPL is trying to flush out the Child, and us with it."

Entry #V-0616

VoxSocial/user/@SaniAbdul

19 November 2047

TRANSCRIPT:

[1] My grandma will be hitting eighty-eight in a few months. If you made that calculation in your head, you'll see she was eight years old when the Nigerian Civil War of 1967—or if we want to be truthful and call it what it was, the Biafran genocide—broke out.

[2] From the way Grandma tells it, they used to live in what is now Bayelsa state, though it was a part of another state in the Niger-Delta region back then, caught halfway between the old Nigeria and the new Biafra. She and her parents had to pack up and run when either of the forces advanced through their village.

[3] If you know anything about the Niger-Delta, the word that comes to mind is *creeks.* A large part of the area is swampy, so this pack-up-and-run really meant lugging their belongings through swamps, wading through murky water filled with feisty reptiles to stay alive and have a hope for tomorrow.

[4] But guess what? It's 2047, there's no civil war, but yesterday, this was my life as well. I literally had to pack up my workstation, put it on my head, and wade through the floods that have made permanent home in Victoria Island, just so I can earn enough to pay rent this month, then do it all over again.

[5] It's crazy how this government has let things degenerate to this level. Look at Port-Harcourt's uninhabitable zones now looking like Chernobyl, filled with sooty air and half their new generations suffering from respiratory problems. When the issue of soot from

gas flaring settling into the city first appeared in the late 2010s, they turned a blind eye and let companies bribe them to flare more gas. Now those same companies have packed up and left Port-Harcourt inhabitants to their fate.

[6] Look at Victoria Island. Any preliminary Environmental Impact Assessment should've told the government that allowing Diekara Industries to literally dredge the ocean and create a private island when the city is already seeing erosion and soil saturation problems would be disastrous. But they must've let those ones pay them and get on with it too. Now, when it rains on Victoria Island, the water doesn't flow anywhere anymore. It just sits there, still.

[7] I used to take the bus or a rideshare to the office. Now, we take canoes. Boatshares if we can afford them. The nearby jetty now has intra-island ferries instead of just the inbound and outbound ones we used to have. The water is thick and murky just like the creeks, and it rises higher and gets more dangerous every day. There have been reported drownings, bodies found floating at daybreak. At least one crocodile was spotted near the now abandoned Federal Palace Hotel. But the government keeps turning a blind eye.

[8] Madness: Isn't that what they call it when you repeat the same thing over and over yet expect different results?

[9] When I got home today, my trousers were wet, my legs speckled with mud from where I had waded in the water. My grandma took one look at me and said, "Eighty years, and you still look like you've just been in the war."

[10] And that, friends, is how the motherland we call Nigeria kills us.

TUOYO

Tuoyo shivered as the words came out of Yekini's mouth. It was Nehikhare all over again.

Back then, the OPL had not been so obvious, so sure. Things had seemed more accidental. *A mishap to the vessel* was the official report, with just enough information to make interested parties satisfied. Of course rumors persisted that it was indeed Children who had attacked the *Centurion,* but their believers—herself included—were made to seem like the crazy ones for suggesting anything otherwise could have happened. And truth be told, the official report had done its work. That layer of doubt about what may have truly happened existed in her mind ever since.

But today, she had no doubts. It was clear. The OPL was willing to murder anyone who was an inconvenience to them. A whole level filled with people—thousands of them. What was a little vessel of scientists and their uncomfortable discoveries?

When the news of Nehikhare came, she had been unable to function properly for months. One thing that kept eating at her: she could have done *something.* She could've gone on the trip with her, probably helped fix whatever it was that had caused the supposed engineering mishap on the vessel. She could've asked her not to go, said that the invitation was too good to be true. She could've been more *active,* more *alive,* more *forceful.* But a loving partner and a life of satisfaction had obscured what life on this tower really was—especially for those who were not as privileged as she was—and it took her too long to realize that.

She was fodder. They all were.

But not today. No more.

Tuoyo snapped out of her daze. Everyone had turned to her.

Fellow engineers, subordinates, even Ngozi. *Foreman,* their faces said, *what do we do?*

"We are going to evacuate," she said without a second thought. "Whether they like it or not. Everyone, prepare for evacuation, *now.*"

"But where to?" someone asked.

Tuoyo peered at the lit lines and arrows and made calculations in her head. They were automatic and baked into the security system, so couldn't have been as quickly shut off by whoever opened the sluice gate. They all likely led to the muster points, which made sense. But not for this situation. Muster was cramped and steamy and was for holding hands and scanning biometrics and calling out unit numbers for headcounts. Perhaps the OPL even *wanted* everyone at muster points. Easier pickings.

"We will not be following the lines," Tuoyo said. "Follow me, everybody." She turned to Yekini. "Help?"

Yekini gave her a definitive nod and faced the group. "You heard the woman. *Move,* people. We have no time."

Everyone followed without hesitation, without concern for order.

Tuoyo headed first for the nearest exit—a stair door. She pulled the handle. Locked. She went straight for the closest elevator doors and punched the buttons. Inactive.

Just as she'd thought, then. The OPL *was* trying to get them specifically to muster. That was one way to be sure no one got out.

She returned to the group. "All right, listen. This level has been sealed off. We need to find another way out of here."

"Sealed by whom?" Ngozi squeaked.

"Ideas, ideas." Tuoyo snapped her fingers. "Quick, quick."

"The submergence vehicle," someone said from behind the line.

"Can't fit everyone," Tuoyo said. "Also needs authorization from the Uppers. *Next.*"

Everyone went quiet, the weight of impending death suddenly hanging heavy. Someone in the back of the line broke down sobbing. Tuoyo's handheld blinked rapidly. Whoever it was was working overtime to decipher her personal code and open that airlock. They could be drowning in minutes.

"The workperson's hatch?" another said.

Tuoyo thought about it for a moment. The hatch opened up on their level, and a steel ladder inside connected their ceiling to the floor of the level above, so that workers could operate in the space between two levels. The catch, though? It was in the south end, so if the doors opened while they were there, they had less than a few seconds before being overrun by incoming water. Even worse, the tower was built in a way that made moving upward without going through certified spaces—like assigned elevators, for instance— virtually impossible. Levels were blocked from every angle. The workpersons couldn't get into the upper level through that hatch if they wanted, and neither could they.

"Hatch will only leave us trapped in the decking," she said, then stopped.

There *was* a third idea. A hatch of another kind.

Tuoyo had always wondered where the garbage that went through the chute ended up. It was common understanding that everything on the tower was carefully recycled, but no one really knew how and where, and no one really asked to see. Tuoyo had always assumed it was all being fed out directly to the sea, but she realized now that Nehikhare would've complained about the new trash destroying the remnant ecosystems she was trying to study.

If the trash was truly recycled on the tower, then it would need a pathway to go from the chutes to wherever it was picked up for recycling—probably down in the lowest of the Lowers, perhaps closer to the turbines, where no one lived. She could wager that everyone's trash ended up there.

And there were two good things about this. One: the chutes were surprisingly large. Part of her role as safety engineer was warning residents to avoid opening them the whole way, and to instead use the smaller trapdoors each chute door was equipped with. The whole chute, when opened, could fit a human person if they angled their body just right. Bad because the refuse closet was almost soundproof, but in this case good because it would make their exit less chaotic.

And two: each chute—and therefore every level—had to be connected by a shared disposal shaft. It was the only way trash could go down.

"*Move!*" Tuoyo said, and went running down the hallway, red light and emergency blares in her wake.

Ngozi followed right behind her, and Yekini corralled the long line of level workers in tow. They went around the curve of the tower and finally arrived at the nearest closet—a small room that held a collection of chutes. Around the corner from where they stood, she swore she could hear the sea straining to get in through the airlock's doors.

"Help me," she said to Yekini. Yekini held one of the chutes open—tagged ORGANIC MATTER—while Tuoyo poked her head in and looked. Darkness beckoned upward, downward.

"I can't see where it goes," Tuoyo said, "but it must have its own maintenance access."

Though she'd never seen maintenance come down to clean chutes in the Lowers, she had seen that happen back when she was in the Midders. Perhaps they couldn't access the chutes from wherever the garbage ended up, so she often saw them enter the shaft from closets such as this, and then somehow climb up or down as needed. Whether they could get into other levels through the same chutes was another matter, but she could only know that if she went in.

First, she took her GripAnything gloves from her belt, slid her hands into them, and turned them on. Then she took her flashlight, tied it to her forehead, flicked it on, and poked her head inside again.

The smell was bad. *Really* bad—clearly maintenance had not been here in a *long* time. But the continuous blaring of emergency alarms and the flashes of light that came into the shaft via the open chute were sufficient to cause her to hustle up.

She turned her light-head each way, sizing up the shaft. *It can take me.* She found a wall—slippery—and plastered her hand on it. The gloves engaged and stuck. *Good.* She put in her other arm and did the same on the opposite wall, then entered.

Her gloves slipped immediately, and down she went with a yelp.

She wasn't falling—not really. The metal walls were just slippery from the errant pieces of garbage lining them, causing her gloves to struggle for purchase. She bucked her knees to reduce her rate of descent, which helped, but her slow-motion journey downward did not stop.

"Tee?" Yekini's head had poked into the shaft. "What's happening?"

"I'm—" She fought the pounding in her temple, the claustrophobia causing her dark cloud to start to gather overhead again. "I'm—slipping."

"What—" Yekini's head retreated, then her boot came through the opening. "I'm coming."

"No, no—" Tuoyo's voice reverberated through the shaft. "Just—wait." She took deep, stinking breaths. *One, two, three. One, two, three. I can do this.* "Go back," she called. "There are no handholds."

But as she said this, her descent came to a stop, and her feet hit something solid. She looked down, and saw it was just the same, like the walls. Like the shaft just stopped. Which made no sense since, well, how did the garbage get through, then?

Then a green light blinked next to her and the base below her whirred open, revealing teeth.

They really were like teeth, the jagged metal edges of the compactor, separating in invitation. Tuoyo pushed her Grip-Anything gloves into the walls with all her might, lifting her legs like a gymnast, so that her boots were only a hair's breadth from the edge of the compactor. She slipped, but not fast enough, thanks to the gloves, without which she would've fallen right through. She held on for a few seconds before the compactor, anticipating her descent but confused about not getting it, blinked twice—amber, amber—then blinked red before shutting immediately, as quickly as it had opened.

Without lowering her legs, she braced her knees on the wall again and sidled up, putting some distance between her and the compactor before looking down again. Now, she could see the serrated teeth where the compactor grabbed at the garbage coming down. And this, perhaps, was why no one had dared go down here unauthorized. They would get swallowed alive in an instant.

But something else caught her eye. There was a panel, where the blinking light had come from. It was right in the middle of the shaft—she must've missed it while coming down. She braced herself again, putting her shoulder into it this time, and pulled upward.

Sure enough, there it was, an access panel, on an almost indiscernible and poorly lit section of the wall, protected from water and other debris by hard fiberglass.

One look, and she knew exactly what she needed to do.

Climbing back up was hard work. Tuoyo found that if she used the corners of the shaft and braced her hand in between, forming a bevel, the GripAnything gloves worked much better on both surfaces than on one alone. She was able to pull herself back to the chute. Yekini helped her back into the garbage closet.

Sounds of rising agitation came through the door from outside. Someone—Ngozi—opened the door, poked his head in.

"Your people are fighting."

"Ugh." Tuoyo headed out to face them, but Yekini held her back.

"I'll go. They're scared, so just pleading with them to be patient while we figure this out might not work. Lemme see if I can use some combination of COPOF authority with that."

She stepped out and Ngozi stepped in.

"Wow." He wrinkled his nose at her clothes. "Rotten in there, is it?"

"You will be rotten when you die down here after they drown us all," Tuoyo said.

"What did I do to you, foreman?" He seemed genuinely perplexed. "Why are you people always angry at me for nothing?"

Tuoyo kissed her teeth and shook her head. "Better get used to the smell because you're going down there yourself."

"Excuse me?"

"Yes." She brushed past him, opened the door, went *psst!* at Yekini, who was still talking to the people, and beckoned her back in. Then she pointed at a random workperson.

"You, your GripAnything, *now.*"

The woman handed the gloves over without hesitation. Yekini came in and Tuoyo shut the door. The three were alone in the closet again.

"There's a compactor separating each level," Tuoyo said, explaining quickly. "I'm guessing every level's trash is compacted before it goes down. It has two openings—one on our side, one at its bottom, which is the next level's side. If we can get past both, we can move down to level eight and come out through its chute's door."

"Phew," Yekini said. "Some good news, finally." She paused. "Why's your face like that?"

"Well, there's more bad news than good news," said Tuoyo. "It uses motion detection. Anyone gets too close . . ." Tuoyo sliced a hand across her neck. "And even if we get past it, there's also the risk of falling. I've climbed many things in my engineer life, and even I almost got eaten by the compactor. It's slippery as fuck down there." She shook her head to clear the memory. "But if we can somehow slide down without falling, open both sides of the compactor at once and enter level eight's shaft without getting killed—all while hoping some garbage doesn't come falling down from the level above, well . . ."

"Fuck," Yekini said.

"There's one piece of good news. An access panel, in the middle. I'm almost a hundred percent sure it's an override to open both sides of the compactor at once—freeze the compaction somehow. I suspect that's what the maintenance workers use.

We can do the same thing, but hold it open long enough for everyone to go down to level eight."

"Then what are we telling all this story for?" Ngozi said, hysterical. "Let's do *that*."

"Well," Tuoyo said, looking to Ngozi. "The override needs an administrator's scan."

He began to take off his wearable. Tuoyo put a hand over his to stop him.

"It's a biometric override," she said. "It has to be *you*."

Ngozi looked pale. "Oh." He shrugged, slowly. "Well."

"Well what?"

"Well. The wearable, I can argue it was stolen and used. My arm? Unless it was cut off or something."

Tuoyo's eyes narrowed. "What are you saying?"

"I'm saying scanning for unauthorized entry using my biometric would be the end of my life—of everything I have worked for."

"*Not* doing that would be the end of your life," Yekini said. "What the fuck! Are you even looking around? Your bosses are going to *drown* us. They know we're down here—they know *you* are down here—and they're going to do it anyway!"

"You don't know that," Ngozi said. "They might have taken control because they're trying to fix it. We should just wait until we know what they're doing, instead of making rash decisions like this. What if they are—"

"Shut up, shut up, shut up!" Tuoyo snapped. "Are you *blind*? You think those people up there care about us down here—*any* of us? They killed my wife. They killed her!"

Silence engulfed the closet and wound tightly around the three. Ngozi bowed his head and looked away. Yekini exhaled audibly.

"You better believe what is right before your eyes," Tuoyo said. "This is who we are in this tower. This is who we have always been. This is what the Pinnacle stands for."

"No." Ngozi was still shaking his head. "This is not—"

"Listen to me," Tuoyo said, a sharp edge she didn't even

know she possessed creeping into her tone. "I'm running out of patience, and we're running out of time. So you *will* go down there with me, and you *will* override the compactor, and you *will* save everybody on this level, or Savior help me, I will strangle you with my bare hands before any water reaches us."

"Then do it," Ngozi said, pointing a finger into her face. "Do it, because *this*"—he opened his arms, gesturing toward the tower—"is the only thing I have. I would rather die than put it all in jeopardy. I've sacrificed too much to get where I am, and I *cannot* throw everything away on the whim of two strangers and some scared—"

Tuoyo growled and grabbed Ngozi's neck.

NGOZI

Stars painted the edges of Ngozi's vision. The engineer's grip on his neck was viselike. She crashed him into a wall, pinned his shoulder blade, clamped him there. He couldn't move or breathe.

Then there was Yekini suddenly between them, her elbow over Tuoyo's outstretched arms, prying her hands off.

"Let . . . him . . . go," she was saying, but was quickly cut off by screams from outside.

Ngozi first felt the coldness at his feet, something tickling against his socks. He shrieked, thought it was a creeping reptile or cockroach at first, but then there was the sound of rushing.

Water poured into the closet from underneath the door, and pooled around all their boots in a cold embrace. Outside, full panic mode had taken hold, and many began to bang on the door.

"Shit, shit, shit," said Tuoyo, splashing backward, releasing Ngozi. She grabbed her handheld. "They've opened the doors!" She tapped at it some more. "They're doing it in small waves to regulate the pressure. We don't have time!"

"Listen, listen!" Yekini was in Ngozi's face now, her breath just as panicky as his. "You're not special. They don't care about you. You're just as expendable as we are. So, you *will* do this. You will do it, or we all die. *All* of us."

She guided him toward the opening, and this time, Ngozi did not struggle or hesitate. Instead, he received the Grip-Anything gloves and pulled them over his shaky hands. Taken over by some kind of autopilot, neither here nor himself. Tuoyo handed him Yekini's boots—"Suction grip, don't fall," she said—and he wore them in zombie-like movements.

The water came thick and fast, and brought with it a green-gray sheen and the odor of sick left unattended too long. The panic outside the closet rocketed—the banging became more insistent. The noises faded, slowly, and Ngozi was elsewhere, back to when he was a small child on this tower.

He didn't know they called here Lowers back then. He didn't even know what the towers were called. All he knew was that they had lived somewhere, and then that place was no more, and they had to move here. He and his sister, Lotachukwu, and a flood of many others like them, braving the journey over sea and spray foam, paying bribes to be smuggled into this new place. Too many bodies, packed illegally into a tiny residential unit. Restless, irritable, aggressive. He remembered little of it. But the images were imprinted in his mind, haunting him over the years. People shitting in the same spots where they rolled up their clothes for pillows. He and Lota, skinny as sugar cane, sucking on orange rinds for sustenance. The constant beating of his heart— the same way it did now—next to a hundred other similar hearts, each one living every day in the fear that they would be discovered and thrown back out to the mercy of the sea.

She used to be bigger than him, back then, Lota. Taller, reedy, a perfect candidate for that sport—basketball, was it? When Pinnacle police finally discovered the unit during a raid, it was Lota who had fought them, fought *for* him. It was she who made sure this flood never swallowed him, never broke his spirit, even if the cost was that it broke hers. It was she who said, *Take me, not him.* And when they pulled her out of that unit, separated him from her and sent him up to be adopted by a midder family instead, he had promised her, silently.

He was going to stay alive and see through this dream—*their* dream, the same dream passed down from their destitute parents, and from their own parents, the ones who had first clawed their way into that other tower. He was going to rise, above the flood, and nothing but death would pry the buoyancy of prosperity from his tightly shut fingers.

So today, even though this flood seemed like it was going to win, he couldn't let it.

"Come on!" a voice echoed from below, jarring him. Tuoyo, already back in the shaft, waiting.

He poked his head inside like he had seen her do, gripped the edge, then climbed in. Water sloshed against the metal panels, echoing within the shaft and growing weightier with increasing depth. When he placed his hands the way Tuoyo said, the grip gloves and suction shoes worked surprisingly well.

"Careful," Tuoyo echoed, "but hurry."

Ngozi's legs started strong, but faltered as he went down, the weight of anxiety and fear combining with the sloshing of increasing water depth outside the chute. He could hear Yekini calling for calm above, struggling to keep the panic reasonable. The water responded by banging harder at the wall panels. He could swear he heard the wall strain, bulge.

"Move!" Tuoyo's voice rang in the shaft.

"Stop yelling!" Ngozi slipped, felt himself falling, but checked his fall. A moment later, Tuoyo's hand gripped his ankle and eased him down.

"There," she said, pointing to a dimly lit reflective panel. Ngozi leaned forward, forearm poised over the panel to open it up.

A drop of water landed on Ngozi's forehead. Then another, and another. A drop landed on his lip—salty. Metal creaked a distance away, ominous.

Above them, Yekini poked her head into the shaft, dripping wet. A splash of water came with her as she waded forward and leaned over the chute.

"You guys better hurry!" she was saying. "They've—"

Something snatched her—and the rest of her words—away.

YEKINI

Yekini stood with Tuoyo's man, Emeka, as the water came in.

He, she surmised, like the small crowd of level 9 workers, paced the breadth of the narrow corridor in high panic, pat-pattering in the water that was starting to rise. He, like every-one here, was trying to get back home to a family that had likely not even heard that something was happening on this level, and would likely be oblivious for a long time to come, depending on whatever story the OPL spun to them if they drowned for sure.

"Time yet?" he was asking.

"You have to calm down," Yekini said. "You've done a good job already today. Don't waste it—let's keep these people in line."

"But me, I need saving too na," he squeaked. Yekini hadn't seen him so agitated since the blood incident, his eyes bulging, face taut with fear.

"I know, I know," she said. "But help me, will you?"

Their attempt to corral the little crowd did not work. Some had already broken off and run through the rising water into units, bolted themselves in. Some curled up into balls, peering into photo images of their loved ones, sobbing without sound. Yekini and Emeka tried everything from persuasion to com-mands to empathizing. *Your boss is doing everything she can, and I trust her,* she told them. *Don't you? She will get us out of here. Now look at me, don't look at the water—look at me!* Between them, they managed to keep only a couple of heads on straight.

Yekini was halfway through with a new candidate when a weighty groan cut the atmosphere, and for a moment, it was as if the Pinnacle had *moved.* Then came even more water, a horrify-ing chorus of it, turning around the hallway, no longer a trickle but a small wave.

Water, Maame used to say to Yekini. *The thing no get enemy.*

Not because water like everybody and everybody like water, no. But because if water decide to mean you, nobody fit fight am.

The wave tumbled Yekini to her buttocks.

This wasn't the big wave she'd been expecting, but Yekini knew now that waiting for that big one was a mistake. *Water no get enemy.* Any one wave might be too strong if let in all at once, and that force could tear this whole tower down. So instead, whoever was doing this had chosen for them a slower death.

Maybe these people were right. Tuoyo and Ngozi needed to get a move on.

"Everyone, stay calm, I'm going to check on them!" she announced, but soon realized she was speaking to a people who had now fully mentally clocked out. Those still around had begun to clamber onto nearby equipment and hang on to pipes. Yekini wasted no further precious seconds, wading back into the closet, poking her head into the hatch. Far down, somewhere, was the glow of Tuoyo's flashlight.

"You guys," she yelled. "Better hurry! They've—"

Water surged into the closet with ferocity, with vengeance, with *intent*. A waist-high green-gray snake, an aqua monster with teeth that ate life and stole breath. The force of the new wave buckled Yekini's knees, dragged her from the hatch. She reached for something—anything—to break her motion, but missed completely and went under.

In the quiet moment before the wave smacked her against the wall and her body went limp, Yekini wondered if this was how the baby in the basket in her dreams felt when the waters swallowed them both.

NGOZI

Water gushed into the shaft from the chute overhead. Ngozi and Tuoyo lost their balance to the weight and force of it. Ngozi struck a shoulder against metal, and a sharp pain brought new stars to his eyes. He blinked into the darkness, nothing but Lota's face swimming before him. But it wasn't her face at all, but the water, now at neck height, reflecting his own back to him.

Tuoyo was thrashing.

"I can't swim!" she cried. "I can't—"

Ngozi breathed in deep, puffed his cheeks, held his breath, and dove in. The dim light was still there, now reflected even more by the water. He jabbed his arm to it and held it there.

The ground below them opened, and the water began to fall through it, slowly at first, like wine out of a bottle. Then suddenly, gushing, a spring unleashed. But the water level did not change significantly, because as much water left the shaft, even more poured in from the chute above.

"Hang on to something!" Tuoyo managed to say once she could get her head above water. She planted her hands on opposite sides of the chute, out of reach of the open compactor, and hung there.

Something else was happening, and Ngozi couldn't tell if this was good or bad. The two panels of the compactor Tuoyo described were both opening up, as expected. But then beyond them, he could see similar compactors opening up as well, water falling through, so far down that they could not even hear the splash when it met its new end.

"I thought you said only level eight!" he screamed to Tuoyo over the sound of rushing water.

"I thought!" came her reply.

What manifested below them was not the safe cocoon he

had imagined they would fall through and be protected by. It was a deep, open throat, beckoning them on to be swallowed.

Water from above gushed harder. It was getting more difficult to hold on. The airlock must have been filled by now, and was probably belching water into the hallways and corridors of level 9. The GripAnything and suction boots struggled to handle the pressure alongside his weight.

"We have to jump!"

He looked at Tuoyo. "You can't be serious!"

"The water will take us down!" she yelled back. "Jump or drown—choose!"

"I can't—" He gazed down, into the darkness, and gulped again. "Once I take my arm off, the compactors will close!"

"Then we take the chance," she said. She looked up as she said it, and he did the same, just as hopeful that Yekini's face might pop back up there again and call to them, join them.

"We should wait for—"

"She's not coming," Tuoyo said, and Ngozi could not determine if it was tears or water that had fallen into her eyes. "Let's go!"

With that, she let go and fell.

Ngozi shut his eyes, thought of Lota.

Go, she had said that night in the dark, police swarming all around them, flashlights in their eyes, firearm muzzles in their faces.

Go, be alive, she had said, before they pulled her and tossed her back into the water.

He took his arm off the panel and let go.

Falling was not as scary as he thought it would be. A rain of water fell with him, streaks of stars in the dark, the shaft above rushing away.

I'm sorry, he thought, as he hit water and was plunged into new darkness.

THE HAND THAT FEEDS IS BUT A FOOT IN DISGUISE

All-Knowing, my friend—

I love how you say *conquer* when you mean *erase*.

Let me borrow from their saying here: they who rewrite stories are doomed to create monsters.

Listen, now, to how they name. Watch them look in the eye something which is them but for one step left, and proclaim, "You are Not." And why? Because a people opened their arms and called sea *sister*?

Friend, your lips say *carve,* but your meaning says *wield.*

What is a monster but one brought to being by many mouths and carried to term by collective bellies? The monster is but he who lives to fight another day, who never falls on her back, but on their many feet, a spider-legged cat. The monster is she who reminds us of the extents of possibility—that there are none. It is them who are neither this nor that nor both nor all nor none.

He is what our eyes cannot see and our ears cannot hear, but whose sweat our tongues can taste and whose breath our skins can feel. It is she who asks us to believe otherwise, to reconsider what is up and what is down. It is them who tell us that we walk on sky and the sea is above us, who prod us to *look, look, look.* It is he who is formed by the tale, created to keep the night away. It is she who stands guard at our doorway, awaiting an invitation.

The monster is the one beneath whom they hide their demons, behind whom they stand and converse with that which is even darker. The monster is the one who says, "Open your eyes. Open, that you may truly see."

So, when you say *nature,* friend, I think: *community.*

Because it was never them against nature. It was never them against monsters. It is always—and always has been—them against themselves.

Entry #A-4035
Start of excerpt.

AFRICARECLAIMED.COM

An Afternoon with Gawl

The indigenous historian opens up on safeguarding our history, the legacies of (neo)colonialism, and the negative effects of modern capitalism on the environment.

by Daniel Onyeama

13 September 2012

Note: This interview was originally carried out exclusively in Hausa, and has been translated to English.

Gawlo Jos, who grew up in a farming community in northern Nigeria, is less than impressed by how indigenous cultivators have frequently been portrayed as environmentally destructive in the wider climate change discourse. Having tilled the land himself, Gawlo Jos is keen to point out that the real exploiters of biological resources are the same people crying over environmental decline.

"They say we kill our forests, we pollute our waters, we ruin the environment for our children," Jos tells me, then chuckles. "Us? With our subsistence farming in small patches for two to three years? My own father even forbade us to disturb roots, not to talk of cutting down trees! Back then, we grew other plants to replace the ground cover we disturbed and resupplied manure to the soil. If we didn't do it, the gods who ruled over soil would cause our crops to fail and our household to fall."

He shakes his head, bites from a kolanut, then holds out a piece to me.

"Look at this fruit, for instance," he says. "We grow it in small portions for use in traditional practices and medicine, yes? But you know who comes here, clears out *our* forests and harvests this to make their cola drinks? The same people saying we are the ones causing yearly floodings in our cities. The same people who say, 'Oh, look at their anti-environmental practices,' then flare poisonous gases into the air and bribe our governments to dump mountains of plastic waste into our rivers.

"Everything is *we, we, we*—and yet we're the ones suffering."

End of excerpt.

NGOZI

When Ngozi came to, someone was dragging him along the ground, but he couldn't see who. He couldn't see, period.

Is this the afterlife the master clerics speak about? he wondered. Had he been found unworthy to partake in the paradise of his ancestors, and instead sent to the underworld cavern?

The dragging stopped, and Ngozi became more aware of his surroundings. He was wet and cold all over, but there was no aching thirst yet, no fire or sulfur eating into his skin.

This definitely wasn't the underworld cavern. He wasn't dead.

Once his hearing returned, there was breathing next to him. He managed to turn his neck—the only part of his body under his control at this point—and a tiny light shone into his face.

The engineer, he realized, when the face behind the light came into view.

Then the memory of events trickled back to him, along with the rest of his five senses. Pain shot through his nose and down to his windpipe. He coughed and, turning to his side, vomited water and snot. His lungs felt too large for his chest, too heavy, and every one of his joints protested. His teeth chattered of their own volition, stinging when touched.

But at least his necklace wasn't gone. He touched his chest and felt the pendant still hanging there.

"Get up," Tuoyo said, pulling him. "We need to find a way out of here."

"Where—" Ngozi coughed, let her help him to his knees. "Where is this?"

"Level six," she said, tapping on a nearby plate bolted to a wall.

LEVEL 6, it did indeed read. That explained the constant humming, small vibrations he could feel all over his body. The same kind he felt the moment he descended into the Lowers, though it was stronger here now that they were likely closer to the turbines.

Over the level's sign, someone had sprayed *DE* and *OMI* and *SIONED,* and then someone had bolted yet another plate that read: RECYCLING.

"We have . . . a whole level dedicated to recycling?" The back of his throat was finally clear enough to make words.

"We don't," Tuoyo was saying. Her wearable glowed as she tapped at it, probably attempting to initiate some sort of contact. He tapped at his own wearable, but felt only a bare wrist.

He peered at Tuoyo. "How did—how are you not injured?"

"Luck," she said. "The water broke my fall better than it did yours. And thankfully so, because one of us had to be awake to get in here through the hatch." She tapped at her wearable again, frustrated. "Whoever rejigged this place did not put in a lot of safeguards. We could've been conveyed straight into the recycler and turned into manure."

The idea caused Ngozi to grow colder. That explained a good many things, like why his chest and back hurt so much, or that banging that was ongoing in his head.

Wait—that wasn't in his head. Tuoyo was turning to look at the direction of the sound too. Whatever recycling thing was going on here had probably hit a snag and was thudding loud enough to be heard all the way over here.

"We need to find that," Tuoyo said, motioning in the direction of the banging. "See if there's a way back up. Come." She didn't offer him a hand.

The abandoned level was dark, sewer-like. Poorly maintained too, because leaks everywhere meant pools of water, in such a manner that they conjoined and formed a never-ending stream. Anything that could have been useful was either rusting or rotting. Now and then, an electrical spark went off somewhere. Somehow, there was still power, a panel or two emitting light. The air was still breathable, and the pressure was still at surface level.

"Batteries," said Tuoyo, answering the unasked question. "Either this place was habitable until recently, or they're keeping it running on basic just for recycling."

She paused. "Did they—" Beneath the faint glow of her wearable, she looked like a ghoul. "Did the OPL drown these people too?"

Ngozi startled as a piece of flotsam grazed him. An adult sandal, one of many floating odds and ends from the people who once lived here. He wondered who once owned it, where they were now. He thought of how useless the sandal was without the other in its pair, and how much in this tower and beyond was the same: dependent on other people and things for their very existence to be effective and meaningful, useless in their absence.

Just like him without Lota, or her without him.

"Don't touch anything," Tuoyo snapped, and Ngozi realized he had absentmindedly been reaching for the sandal.

"Unless you love getting electrocuted," Tuoyo said. "This whole place is a hazard."

They waded in the dark, with nothing but the failing light of Tuoyo's wearable to guide them, and the drip-drips of water for accompaniment. It stank of mold and decay, the way water left too long always did. Every now and then, Ngozi heard the proud buzzing of mosquitoes, a sound he recognized from his time as a refugee, one he hadn't heard in a long time—insects didn't fare so well in the higher altitudes of the Midders and Uppers. It took him back, in flashes, to a time and place very much like this one. The details were a blurry smorgasbord of sound and imagery, none of which he could interpret in words, but all of which he could interpret in feeling.

He shrugged them off, focusing on the sights around him. Vestiges of those who once lived here. Metal parts of some larger apparatus or equipment, sticking out of the walls or floors, skeletal remains of their former selves. Open drain holes, the grates once used to keep water from pooling on the floors now gone.

"Do you think—you think level nine looks like this right

now?" The solemnity in his voice surprised him. "It must've been horrible, whatever happened here."

"You think?"

He couldn't tell if she was being sarcastic or not.

"I think they converted this place to hide whatever they did here." She spoke through gritted teeth, angry, but not at him. "And it's the Children who are supposed to be the barbaric ones."

Ngozi wanted to say the OPL must have had a reason. This was something he truly believed—or at least once had. But then what had happened up there had happened, and he wasn't so sure anymore.

One thing he knew now, though: whatever semblance of a life he'd had; whatever plans for ascendancy or favors to be curried, he could toss all of that through a porthole now, out to sea.

"Was this inevitable?" he found himself asking aloud. "What they did—is that what they wanted all along?"

"I don't know."

He peered into her face, lit by the side glow of the wearable. "Listen, I just want you to know that . . . I'm sorry. For Yekini. Back there—"

"Let's not." Tuoyo did not look at him. "Let's just . . . not."

Things began to get newer, lighter, brighter, as they approached the recycling units. The area was completely untouched by the darkness and water of everywhere else.

The loud bangs were closer now. They did not sound at all like regular recycler operations. They sounded like someone—or *something*?—beating against a panel, inside the wall or outside it. A damaged piece of equipment, maybe?

"What the fuck is that?" Tuoyo swung her wearable's light left to right, seeking anything to use as a weapon. She found a metal bar and grabbed it. For a moment, Ngozi wondered if he should find one for himself, then decided he was useless with weapons anyway.

Another bang.

"Someone is trying to get into this level," Tuoyo said. "Some-one . . . knows we're here."

Ngozi's mind flashed through possibilities. The OPL had quickly discovered their escape and was here to retrieve them. The Children had not been flushed out, but had followed them down here instead.

Bang.

"Should we run?" Ngozi asked.

Tuoyo tilted her head, a moment's pause. Then:

"No." Her face tightened. "There's nowhere to go. And I'm tired of running." She stepped forward.

"Wait—what are you doing?"

"Orbiting my head like a rain cloud," she was saying, and Ngozi was unsure if she was speaking to herself or to him. "Time to face it."

As Ngozi watched her advance toward the pounding, he realized this moment was a microcosm of what his life was going to be like going forward. Whether he stayed in place or moved forward, he was doomed either way. There was no going back to the life of old, and there was no plan for how to move forward. The only way to proceed was to, well, *proceed.*

He grabbed his pendant, squeezed it tight. *At least there's hope in forward,* Lota used to say, grinning as they chewed on orange rinds stolen from waste bins. Perhaps, if there was ever a good time to listen to her, it was now.

TUOYO

The banging was coming from inside the wall.

Tuoyo had spent enough time as an engineer to recognize the sound of someone working from inside of something. As she stood before the panel she'd identified as the errant one, her safety officer's brain wanted her to give the panel some distance—*Minimum approach of ten feet to utility components.*

But the storm that had been building up in her had finally taken hold, blown past every sense of self-preservation. Now, she was driven solely by rage and heart, by breath and ache. Everything she knew and loved had been gobbled up by a system determined to squeeze the life out of her, out of the residents of level 9, out of people on this tower who were doing nothing but simply trying to survive.

She was done playing by its rules. It was time to play by hers.

Tuoyo stepped forward, braced her metal pole against the wall panel like a pry bar, and leaned on it.

The panel groaned, fell and gave way to darkness.

Recognition came slowly. Tuoyo saw eyes, nostrils, a mouth. Gills, covered; a . . . fin, maybe? Webbed fingers?

A trick of the darkness, she thought. Perhaps despondency had exerted such weight on her mind that she was seeing more than there was. She rose, calmly, and turned her forearm so the light of her wearable was pointed into the darkness.

The Child crept out of the hole, slowly.

All of these years, Tuoyo had fantasized about what exactly she would do to the first Child she encountered. She had planned it meticulously. First, she would pull out the police-grade folding knife she always carried in the hip pocket of her khaki trousers, so small it could be covered completely by her fist once flipped open, with only a sliver of blade peeking out. She had practiced flipping it thousands of times, so that the motion had become one with her wrist: expose the blade, index finger behind the axis, *flip*. The blade would come erect, and like she had practiced on the dummy in her unit, she would lunge as quickly as her body would allow.

In her research about the Children, she had considered all the possible dangers of an encounter and narrowed down the three easiest methods to incapacitate one. The trusty jugular, if they were close enough to human physiology. The gills, wherever they were placed—she assumed they had some if they breathed underwater. Bonus points if they were located on the face and forward-facing. And if all else failed, the eyes, whatever form they took. And then, while the Child bled out, hopefully horrifically, she would watch. She would sit there and smile, and think, *Take that, killer. Take that for taking away the love of my life.*

It surprised her, therefore, when in this moment, she found herself unable to move, not even to feel for the zipper of her pocket to check if the knife was still there. And that moment she wasted was all it took to change everything.

The Child plopped out of the wall, wet and gleaming, and pulled something—*someone*—behind them. Tuoyo did not recognize Yekini at first, seeing only a dripping lump. Then she spotted the woman's locs and her breath caught in her throat.

Ngozi came up behind her and, taking in the sight, froze as well.

Both stood there, eyes shifting from Yekini to the Child to Yekini, hoping for some movement—not from the Child, but from Yekini's closed eyes. *Open,* they prayed, *or even just flicker.* The Child, whom they were yet to catch a proper glimpse of in the dim light, was of the same disposition: one eye on them, another on Yekini. All three stood, watching, waiting.

Carefully, the Child reached across, turned Yekini over, and ripped off her wet, heavy bulletproof vest in one swift motion. Now Tuoyo could see the little rise-and-falls of the woman's chest. A wave of relief washed over her, so powerful that Tuoyo sank to the floor, knees unable to hold her weight. A hope she hadn't felt in a long time filled her chest, warm and bright.

As she knelt there, watching the Child, who in turn squatted there and watched her and Ngozi, Tuoyo realized what the Child was doing: *waiting*. It had made its move, and now was waiting for her to decide if she was going to be friend or foe.

She was going to have to make a decision, to choose: for herself, for Yekini, and maybe for the future of the Pinnacle.

But she never got to make that decision, because in that very moment, Yekini coughed and opened her eyes.

YEKINI

Yekini was back at the ark.

She knew, in this instant, why Maame had told her this story. It had never really been the story of the ark. It was, in truth, Maame's story, the one of how she had lost her own child to the sea.

I was young, naive, Maame would say, staring into space, then look at Yekini out of the side of her eye, in that way that said, *I was just like you.* Sometimes, she would say: *I should've saved them; I should never have saved myself.* Sometimes, she would wail, long and hard and out of the blue, and then stop just as suddenly. Every now and again, she would ask meaningless questions, like: *What does it mean to live for yourself?*

The only thing that always made sense was when she would look Yekini in the eye and say: *My debt is paid, because I at least saved you.*

Yekini was back at the ark, and Olókun and Noah and Sekhmet and Uta-napishtim and Deucalion and Waynaboozhoo and Manu were there, their hands outstretched as one, insistent. Yekini looked down at hers, but saw nothing—no basket, no baby. Instead, she was underwater herself, being taken away, breathless. Ears and nose clogged, swallowing saltwater and stink. Her brain feeling like it would burst; her forehead on fire from all the water shooting up her nose.

But the ark's keeper, now a composite of all ark keepers, kept following, asking her to just reach out, just take a chance on them.

So she took it. She reached out.

Their grip was strong, stronger and firmer than she'd ever expected. She peered closer and realized they weren't an ark keeper at all, but something different, *someone* different.

Then their strong arms gripped her body, and she could not remember anything for a long time.

Yekini opened her eyes.

For a lengthy moment, a certain kind of panic gripped her, one where she thought her life was only going to be darkness, a void, an inability to perceive and feel and remember. The weight of her time under pressed on her, a time that had felt like years or centuries. Now, she was yanked from that world, from its crushing breathlessness, and the first thought that came to her was: *Never again.*

Then she looked up, and immediately wanted to go back under.

The eyes before her were not of a kind she had ever seen. Translucent, almost lifeless, but not quite. They did not blink—they were lidless—and did not shift, but stayed wide open, as if perpetually scared. Yet there was no fear in these eyes, only interest, and perhaps a kind of waiting, an anticipation, a hope.

She was staring into the eyes of a Child.

Yekini was a young girl when she'd seen her first image of the OPL's version of what a Child would look like. The broadcast—*If you see something, say something!*—had interrupted her children's masquerade puppetry programming hour. She didn't remember asking Maame what kind of masquerade puppet that was, though Maame, through her melodramatic and heavily augmented stories, insisted she had.

In Maame's version of events, she had sighed and looked at this little girl, too little to know anything about the world before her, about history and ancestry and guiding spirits, about governments and a little thing called propaganda, and said: "Turn off the screen."

Maame had proceeded to sit Yekini on the unit's soft carpet and, as she often did when a teaching moment presented itself, tell a story. But this time, it was not a story. It was these words:

"What is the color of this seat?" she asked, pointing to a nearby couch.

Yekini looked at it, confused. "Red . . . ?"

"And what if I told you it wasn't? What if I told you it's black?"

"But I know it's red," Yekini said.

"Only because I told you so," Maame said. "And because everyone else around you has supported this understanding. But if I had told you it was black, and everyone else in this tower agreed with me, and we had a collective agreement that this color was going to be black for us all, what then would be the true color of this seat?"

This question confused Yekini, and she offered no response.

"If you went your whole life understanding—and believing— that this seat was black, would that change the color of red as it exists in the world, or would it change it only in your eyes?"

"Maame, I don't understand," Yekini whimpered.

"Listen, child," Maame said. "Every story you believe, that you incorporate within the self, decides who you are. And the greatest weapon against freedom is to believe stories that plant a seed in your heart yet have no place growing there."

Yekini remembered simply resigning herself to sitting there and listening, since all of this was getting too complex for her young brain. (Maame insisted she had been rapaciously attentive.)

"Maybe that thing you saw is a puppet masquerade, or maybe it is not. What matters is that it is a part of who we are and have always been, whether from the civilizations before or those of now. And, dear child, you cannot hate your own history. To hate your history is to hate yourself." Maame paused. "Open your eyes."

Yekini had forgotten all about this exchange, but in this moment, staring at the first Yemoja's Child any eyes in the tower had seen, Yekini realized something was happening with her slow and calculated response: she was taking Maame's advice.

She was opening her eyes.

YEKINI

After she was done vomiting; after she'd sat up, regained her balance; after she'd felt the cold and wet embrace of someone she recognized to be Tuoyo; after Ngozi, shivering beside her, said, *You're alive!*; after Tuoyo, between glances at the Child sitting patiently and quietly at a distance, explained where they were and how they got there; Yekini turned her gaze to the Child and asked the only question that mattered in the moment.

"Who are you?"

The Child waited. Waited for her to weigh the gravity of the question, to understand that a response was a hand reaching across the divide, an invitation to allyship and camaraderie. Only after this was established did the reply come, in a voice that trilled:

I am Omíwálé.

The response arrived with a tremor, passing through all three of them so that they shuddered as one. Yekini *felt* the words arrive in her head, a bird perching softly. The Child's lips had not moved an inch, and Yekini's ears had not heard anything other than the constant humming around them. But all three had received the same message, loud and clear, as if it had been spoken.

"Whoa," said Ngozi. "How—?"

"The water that comes," Yekini said.

"This is . . . ?" Tuoyo, kneeling beside Yekini, looked woozy. "What . . . ?"

"The name," said Yekini, surprising herself by how naturally she was taking all this in. Perhaps Maame's stories had finally delivered on their purpose, sowing seeds and bearing fruit in her mind in a way that prepared her for a situation exactly like this one.

"The name what?" Ngozi was saying. "Did everybody hear that? Did you—"

"That's what it means—Omíwálé," Yekini continued. "It's Yoruba. *The water comes home.*"

She turned back to the Child, who seemed to be smiling at her recognition, although she couldn't be sure. She didn't know how to interpret a face that she didn't understand.

"We have been visited by water once before," she said. "It did not end well."

The Child nodded, a motion she could finally understand.

You see the words, said Omíwálé, *but what you struggle with is understanding. I have not come to cause havoc, but to separate into small recognizable patterns, so that, piece by piece, you may understand the whole.*

"What is this?" asked Tuoyo, rising, stepping back. "What is happening?"

"I don't like parables," Ngozi was saying. "We should just ask it yes-or-no questions."

"I suggest we use *they* for now, until we're told otherwise," said Yekini. "You can't use *it* for a person."

"A *person?*" Tuoyo said, but then as soon as she said it out loud, realized what it sounded like, and promptly swallowed the rest of her words. Ngozi did the same.

Yekini returned to the Child. "*Water comes home.* Is this home? If so, who are your people? Do you come on behalf of them? Are you a messenger?"

The Child seemed to relax in posture now, realizing this was going to be more of a discussion than a confrontation.

You may call me a messenger, though that will not entirely be correct, they said. *My people and yours are of the same root—we are simply different branches. This used to be home once for us, as it is for you now. But we—once the perished—we are now the people of the Queen Conch. Once sold to sea for death, but instead found life within the waves. We are those who have been looked kindly upon by our foremother Yemoja, god of all waters. She reached into her treasures and pulled from it the Quickening, from which we have been gifted this life that was once denied us. But today, I have chosen to return here, to where I belong just as I belong beneath the waves.*

"And what is the purpose of your return?"

Refuge. For myself, but also for others like me.

"Refuge from what?"

My own people. Just as you now seek refuge from yours.

The three looked at one another.

"Why are your own people hunting you?" asked Tuoyo. "Are you dangerous?"

Dangerous is a name for things we do not understand. I am a thing that is not understood, both among my people and among yours.

"Why?" asked Ngozi. "Because you can breathe above and under water?"

The Child angled their head. *You have guessed right. Like you, we contain multitudes, and sometimes, such an existence causes discomfort. Discomfort, untamed, twists into hate. Hate leads to you and me sitting here and talking to each other.*

"You are aquatic, yes? You're not *supposed* to breathe above water."

You have learned a great many things, said Omíwálé, *but the natural world does not care what you have learned. It moves and changes of its own accord, whether you believe it is* supposed *to or not. We are all given life by something or the other—us, just by the Quickening. We may decide* who *we become, but none of us has full control of* what *we become. I am but one of many manifestations of the self—and just like land and sea and other forces, my body pines for what it used to be, and dares to re-create a semblance of its former self. But the body is malleable, and nature is fallible, and sometimes, that creates in-betweens, an either-or and neither-nor. I, and many others like me resurrected by Yemoja's Quickening, are in-betweens. This is not our choice. And yet, we are doomed to be constantly misunderstood, at home and beyond.*

The Child rose then, gaunt, well over six feet, and said: *You ask why I have come here? I come seeking understanding, but I also come bringing it.*

Yekini rose slowly, helped up by her counterparts. They did not look stricken anymore, or disgusted, or vengeful. But they moved warily, which she could understand. The most important thing was that they did not look like they wanted to murder this Child, who had saved her life when they could have chosen not to. She felt responsible, in this way, for protecting Omíwálé, if only to repay the favor. That was a good place to start, at least.

"We do not wish harm or destruction on you," said Yekini. "At least, not us three. But I'm not sure how we can help you in your quest. As you can see, we are incapacitated ourselves."

Understandable, said Omíwálé. *But you must remember: it is fate that has brought us together, not me. Each one of us here has somehow tasked themselves with making our world better than it is—helping a people divided by time and tales come together. What are we if not called and chosen?*

Yekini did not believe in such things, but as she listened to the Child, the images from her recurrent dreams came to mind. *What are we if not called and chosen?* Was there something out there calling to her, shuttling images into her mind, insistent? Was this something she was called to do?

She should have died up there in level 9. Somehow, she was alive. Perhaps she had been kept alive because her work wasn't done yet. Perhaps this was her one true purpose in this tower all along.

"What do you need from us?" she asked.

Take me to one who can offer the stories of the Queen Conch to all.

"The Queen Conch?"

The Child reached somewhere within its body—the idea of a fish's pocket felt deeply alien to Yekini, so much so that she struggled not to retch. Out of this pocket came a seashell, dry and untouched by any kind of wetness. Smooth and pink like a tongue on one side, brown and coarse like a tortoise's back on the other.

Holder of stories, said Omíwálé. *Teller of tales.*

"So, you want us to give that to the prime?" asked Ngozi. "I doubt Diekara will want to hear anything from us after what happened up there. Or you, for that matter, seeing as you started all this."

"Do they even know we're still alive?" said Tuoyo. "They must think we're dead, and that all evidence of what happened on level nine is gone."

No, you misunderstand me, said Omíwálé. *I am not asking for whoever presents themselves as your leader. I ask for that which is your voice, one who neutrally relays what is offered.*

"Like . . . software?" asked Yekini.

I do not know what that is. Perhaps you should try it and see for yourself.

Yekini frowned. "Try what?"

Avail yourself to the Queen Conch of our foremother. The Queen Conch will reveal her secrets to an eye that fears not to see, ears that listen willingly, a tongue that speaks no violence, nostrils that parse before inhaling, digits that crave connection, and a heart that holds no prejudice. Perhaps you may qualify, and witness its secrets for yourself, understand what needs to be done.

Yekini received the seashell from the Child. It was cool to the touch, larger than she'd envisaged—it far outsized her palm—and so smooth on the pink side that it was like a newborn in her hands. She had never handled a newborn herself, but thought the experience would be just as sublime as this: standing in the presence of that which seemed little, but in the grand scheme of things, whose possible impact on the future was greater than anything her mind could conjure.

So she put the cold, dark tunnel of the Queen Conch to her eye.

Origin; Or, upon Placing the Queen Conch to Eye

Do you know the story
of how we learned
to walk first
and again?

On the seabed, it is understood.

Fin to arm, tail to feet,
gills, nostrils, scales and skin

and soon, soon,
limbs.

First, paddle; then, waddle.
Legs four, then two.
Stand.
Breathe.

Many names, you called us:
    Tiktaalik
    Walking Fish
    Mami-Wata
    Yemoja's Child.

Did you wonder
if the name for us
was the name for you,
    Human?

Mutation; Or, upon Placing the Queen Conch to Nostril

It begins with the smell of evil. Hearts filled with greed, the putrid odor of malice spilled oversea. Next come the cries of anguish, voices of strangers-kin, stuffed into the belowdecks, one stacked over the other as sacks. And so they are thrown overboard, cargo, freefalling.

Mama Yemoja has since put the Queen Conch to ear, and her ears bleed from the agony above. She puts the Queen Conch to nose and is stung by the sweat-salt of those who placed the crying ones in chains. Her heart sinks to the ocean bottom, and she lets out a wail of shared pain. It goes forth a strong wave, reverberating across the ocean, forcing her discomfort on the waters, so that nothing made by human hands can witness that and live to tell.

Therefore she feels a duty to the criers in chains, when their bodies slap the water. Each she cradles in her arms, singing soft lullabies. But alas, their lungs are insufficient, giving out faster than they can exhale. So, into the depths she takes them, one by one, laying their heads to rest. But rest they do not, convulsing, fragile bodies rejecting the darkness of the deep. Mama Yemoja dips into her treasures, then, at last gasp, and brings forth the Quickening.

When the Quickening—that smooth, holy globule of air and life and water and shine—touches them, their bodies respond to the tune of a thousand years per second. Where the Quickening finds usefulness, it retains. Where it finds deficiency, it provides. It erases and commingles and brings forth anew all at once, so that, soon, their chains are broken, and when they open their eyes, they can breathe and see and hear and feel and be free again.

So are born the first Children of Yemoja.

We build cities from the memories we can piece together, slivers of our old lives oversea no longer fully grasped. We build for those who are cast afresh from the bowels of ships, for there are many more as the centuries unfold. We build for children that never survive, for soon they are snatched by predators undersea. We build, but we are never safe.

The bodies stop coming. We listen, through the Queen Conch our foremother has left us. We peek over the surface, for as long as our new lungs will allow, to see what has become of oversea. Time passes. We grow old. We peek over the surface. Oversea has changed. The bodies stop coming. It is time to return.

We preserve our history in the Queen Conch. We abandon our cities, and leave the Quickening behind. We know the stench of a human heart weighed by avarice. We know its stain never washes away. We know that, soon enough, strangers-kin will need it again.

Our ancestors ventured out to the Atlantic and tumbled into the ocean, bodies slapping the water. When the Atlantic comes to Lagos, the water finds us at home and slaps us there.

The Queen Conch seeks us out, or we find it, we are not sure which. Perhaps it was lonely, and called us to itself, whispering the stories of our ancestors into our death-wakes. It leads us to the Quickening, and we are reawakened, rekindled, reforged. It goads us to place it to ear, to eye, to nostril, to tongue, to touch— and we do. Soon, we are inundated with yet another flood, this one of cries and mourning and chains and suffering, but also of rebirth, of knowledge, of lineage, of hope. We are situated.

We rebuild the cities. We learn the secrets of undersea, but also those of oversea, for we possess a firmer grasp of who we are, now. We thank our ancestors for the guidance given. We venerate them and ask for help when we need it the most.

But most importantly, we remember. We remember the faces of those oversea, who turned deaf ears to our cries and offered us up to the waves. We bide our time. We wait for each moment, after they have become comfortable and dare to come down and venture upon our waters. And we savor it, the waiting, because we are filled by it, as we are filled, too, when we pounce.

YEKINI

Fuck.

YEKINI

"Take . . . *them* into the Midders?" Tuoyo scoffed. "Are you *kidding* me?"

Yekini, fresh from inhaling the secrets of the Queen Conch, bristled with verve and vitality. She'd at once shunted her comrades into a corner, away from the Child, and revealed the plans that had come to her in the small eternity she'd spent falling through time and tale, history and future.

"What you're asking is madness," the engineer said. "We can't even get into the Midders on our own, not to talk of with a *Child*!"

"Yes, I know it sounds absurd," said Yekini. "But hear me out—we only have to do two things. If we can somehow get back up to level sixty-six, I can hide them in my unit. Then, it's just a matter of getting the Queen Conch across to, I don't know, someone, something?" She turned to Ngozi. "You can help us with your access—"

Ngozi was already shaking his head. "Agent Yekini, I'm happy you're alive. Truly. But I've sacrificed enough already. I think this—here—is where my sacrifices end."

"Look at us," said Yekini, stepping back to regard them. "Not a single one of us who stands here has not already sacrificed something. We have all lost something to the OPL." She pointed to Tuoyo. "You want to tell me your spouse would've asked you to abandon this?"

"Don't you dare—" Tuoyo started.

"Admit it. You know it's true." To Ngozi, she said: "You, too. I know you pretend you don't care about anything, but I've seen you whisper to yourself." She pointed at the necklace tucked into his shirt. "I've heard you talk to that when you think no one's listening. I know you've lost something or someone. I'd bet you lost it to this tower too."

Ngozi bit his lip, shut his eyes. Yekini pressed it home.

"You think they would ask you to turn your back on someone in need? On someone who needs help in a way that they once needed help?"

Ngozi shook his head. "I promised I'd stay alive."

"Then stay alive!" Yekini went over to Ngozi and placed her hands on his shoulders. "They wanted you to make life better for yourself, yes, but also for others like you, like them. All those people in level nine—they were just like us. They had family, loved ones. We walk away from this, we're saying their deaths, their sacrifices, their wishes don't matter. So, we *live*. We live for them, and for ourselves." She held up her arms. "Fate has handed us, those who *lived,* an opportunity. What are we if not called and chosen?"

Tuoyo and Ngozi glanced at one another. There was not much shared camaraderie there. But there was shared understanding and a shared recognition of their place in the possible future that awaited.

"And you?" Tuoyo said, tilting her chin at Yekini. "What did the OPL take from you that has you pumped up like this?"

Yekini struggled to make it make sense in her head, but when it did come together, it was easy to enunciate.

"Dreams," she said, then turned to Omíwálé. "We'll do it."

ASK NOT WHAT IS, BUT WHAT ISN'T

Dearest All-Infinite—

I've been thinking about
        spaces
since we last spoke; about
        spirit
in pauses between; about
        stories
in words left unsaid.

We are not watchers on a hill but
        the watched,
beady eyes from below
        stabbing.

We dare not answer, but
cup hands behind ears;
        listen!
a cry for help
from the end of the world.

Recollection; or upon Placing the Queen Conch to Skin, to Tongue

The ritual of recollection starts with a roiling in the belly, a hankering, a gathering of desire. Faces stricken, bubbles of anxiety, sweat-salt on lips licked. Fins tucked, belts cinched, offspring gripped tightly. This is the waiting before the coming.

The drums begin to talk. Palms smack stretched drumskin smacks our earpits. The Heralds, those who have long held the tales of our forebears so they may never be lost, open their lips, and our histories wash over us. The Heralds call, and the responses come to us and we *know*.

This is our forebears in one body, singing.

Here come the departed, a shoal of ghosts, parting the waters like sword. Here comes the swish of robes that once belonged to spirits who now lie beneath, the combs that once held their hairs aback.

This is our forebears in one body, dancing.

What is the weight of grief, passed from body to body, a wound shuttled across time and skin? What is the weight of a sore that festers for generations? This, and many other questions, prowl the dreams of the Heralds.

How did you come to be so fragile, you? How did you become unable to bear this weight on behalf of your people, to pass on what it needed, to hold in the stories of their existence, without which they will succumb to slow death?

Do you not come forth from god? Beneath this gill and fin and scale, this seaweed ensnaring your limb, this glare of the oversea sun in your eye—are you not, under that skin, divine? Were you not once a conduit between the seen and not-seen, existing on a

line and a line alone? Were you not once both touched and un-
touchable? Were you not once, the world?

The questions prowl and prowl, seeking answers.

When the answer comes, it is quiet and uncluttered: *the weight of
grief is not a weight for bodies.*

So, it is spoken and agreed: the tales of the Children of Yemoja
must be tucked into the Queen Conch. If a body wishes to be reminded, the Queen Conch may be retrieved, and will freely reveal
her secrets to:

—eyes that fear not to see;
—ears that listen willingly;
—tongues that speak no violence;
—nostrils that parse before inhaling;
—digits that crave connection; and
—a heart that holds no prejudice.

Never again will these burdens be placed on an unwilling
body. Now, a body must choose for itself if it will bear this weight
of memory and understanding.

YEKINI

Tuoyo already had a plan for a way back up.

In the next fifteen minutes—or what felt like it—Yekini would come to realize why Tuoyo had been level 9 foreman. It was easy, at first glance, to look past her semi-aloofness, consider her un-noteworthy. Yet, so far, it was she who had devised a solution to save them three—four, if they counted the Child. Now, as she opened her mouth to explain a plan to get them topside, Yekini realized that this unassuming woman was going to be their best chance at survival, and possibly the OPL's worst nightmare.

"The recycling system seems to be in five parts," Tuoyo said. "*Collection*—that's where we came through. That's followed by *separation* and *breakdown,* where the inbound material is, well, separated and broken down. Like we would've been if we hadn't got out early." She grunted at the memory of the near miss. "Anyway, after that is *reformation,* which we can't see because it's happening inside that giant processor you see there. But if you look closely, that's *transportation* right there, where the final goods come out."

They stood in front of the gleaming machinery, squinting at where Tuoyo pointed. The recycling system had clearly been built after the level's demise. It was a pristine and functional piece of gadgetry, a new arm attached to a rotten body.

Tuoyo was pointing to a platform where the automated system dumped large cubes of various kinds of output, of which there were exactly five: mixed paper, glass, mixed plastic, metal, compost. All went into hardboard crates before being transported to their respective levels for use.

"We need to get on one of those crates and follow it to its final destination," Tuoyo said. "Wherever that is."

"Aren't those boxes being squashed?" Ngozi cupped his hand

against the glass that separated them from the unit. "Are *we* going to get squashed?"

Tuoyo shrugged. "No clue. But unless you have a better idea . . ."

"Do we have any guesses where these end up?" Yekini asked.

"I know compost goes to Agric," said Ngozi. "That's level thirty-three, right on the surface. So maybe we don't want to follow *that* crate."

"Metal, plastic and glass will likely go to smelting and manufacturing," Tuoyo said. "Which means somewhere in the Lowers. So that's a no as well. Which means we're left with paper, which goes to—"

"Level sixty-two," Yekini said.

Tuoyo and Ngozi turned to her.

"I was there once," she said. "COPOF business. You know the Uppers still use paper for discreet documentation? They get it from a small mill, a tiny, uninteresting unit on sixty-two." She pointed at the latest paper crate, machine grips preparing it for transport. "Maybe those go directly from here to that unit."

"So we follow it up there," said Tuoyo. "And then what?"

"And then go down to my unit." Yekini pointed to Ngozi. "Or yours."

"Where do you live?" Ngozi asked.

"Fifty-seven."

"Agh, you'll be closer," he said. "I'm in the seventies."

"And what about them?" Tuoyo pointed at Omíwálé. "We may be able to fool patrols that I'm a midder for a hot moment, but that one shows their face and we won't last a second."

Yekini put a finger to her chin. "I may have a solution."

The solution was for Omíwálé to hide inside the crate. Seeing as they had managed to squeeze themselves through a sluice gate and wall opening, making themselves comfortable within the crate should be easy. It helped that the crates were made of hardboard and contained only light packing material.

The hard part, when they'd finally agreed, was watching Omíwálé squeeze themselves into the crate. They bent their body this way and that, twisted it as if they had a rotating spine, as if they had a malleable body. The movement felt so alien that Yekini found herself queasy just from watching, a rumbling in her stomach asking to be let out. She was sure, now, that this was how they likely had folded themselves throughout this tower.

On another day, she would have called Omíwálé the word that clung to the edge of her mind: *monstrous*. But once they'd finally settled into the crate, locked inside, another word came to her: *victim*. Non-tower dweller or not, the Child was simply yet another victim of the Fingers and their decades-spanning legacy.

But as fate would have it, the mantle had fallen on her to try to make sure that this legacy did not extend into the future and destroy the lives of tower citizens yet to be born.

This time, thought Yekini, *everyone gets on the ark.*

YEKINI

The ride up was rocky but uneventful. All three of them squatted atop the crate, which rested on a platform that went up its own narrow hoistway. They clung to the edge as it rocked upward, clangs echoing around them in the shaft. Yekini, claustrophobic, kept imagining another crate or platform descending from above and crushing them.

She shut her eyes, wondering what her colleagues back at CO-POF would think of her little expedition now. Would Monsignor think this was what she deserved for always asking to leave her desk? Would Nabata sense something amiss, especially if this all went sideways and the OPL inevitably came up with a story to explain her disappearance? Perhaps they were already putting one together now.

She thought of Maame, who she knew would never believe a word out of the OPL's mouth. Maame would be, to her, what Tuoyo was for her wife—someone who would keep on believing.

The platform ground to a halt, settled the crate onto a conveyor belt, and eased them sideways into level 62. The paper mill, when the belt deposited them in it, was pitch dark. Once they'd groped around, bumped into obstacles—shelves, equipment, more crates—they found a switch and some light.

The unit was much smaller than Yekini had envisaged. There were signs of a small workforce—three, at most—and a work day ended: stacks of paper only half sorted; the lingering smell of sweat; abandoned cups with dregs of beverages still in them. For a supposedly secret location, it was quite a mundane affair.

"Stairs?" asked Ngozi, once they had found their bearings. "Out of sight is better, right?"

"Not with that weight," said Tuoyo, nodding at the crate.

"So, what, we just . . . walk down the hallway?"

Tuoyo shrugged. "Better with a crate than with a Child, right?" She looked to Yekini. "What do you think?"

Yekini had been thinking about this too, on their ride up. Up here, the levels were all designed in the same manner. If she was to guess, they had landed in the work wing, which meant that upon exiting this room, the freight elevators would be at either end of the curved hallway. How *far* away was a whole other question, but she assumed a relatively short walk to the nearest one, and a short ride to level 57 after. They could be back in the safety of her unit within minutes.

"If we move fast enough," she said, "and if we don't run into any patrols . . ." She let that hang, staring at the crate. "You think they're okay in there?"

Ngozi tapped on the crate and put his lips next to it. "Say you're okay if you're okay."

I'm okay, came the response from inside.

Ngozi shivered. "Egh. I will *never* get used to that."

"So," Tuoyo was saying, "in plain sight, then? Risky. But I was also thinking"—and here, she turned to Ngozi—"we have you and your almighty status. If we run into trouble, you can simply, yunno, do your thing."

"And what is my *thing*?"

"Look at me, senior man," Tuoyo said in a poor impression of Ngozi. "I shall tell you what to do."

Ngozi shook his head. For once, he seemed chagrined by his status.

"Ridiculous," he said, then nodded at the crate. "Shall we?"

Level 62, overall, was quite similar to other levels Yekini had been to. Each unit here had its own distinctive look, every owner doing something to mark the territory as theirs. In the way of many midders, like those on Yekini's level, most had pinned their names to their doors, or had some sort of marker or identifier or decoration. No one wanted to be *Unit 6201* or *Resident 09385*. They wanted to be *Sunday two units down* or *Minna around the bend*. Some markers of identity were more elaborate: intricate designs or paintings of families or forerunners or other people of importance; in some cases, there was artwork that covered the unit's whole front door. Others were simpler: just a name or a quote (*If it's meant to be, it'll be*) or a sign announcing something (*Just got married, whoo!*) or even nothing. Just the plain, usual, living-in-this-tower-until-I-die existence.

One thing was clear, though: they were not in a work wing at all. They were in a residential wing.

"We'll be fine," Yekini whispered, when this became evident. "Just act like you're on regular OPL business or something."

The residents of level 62, however, did not make it easy. Their eyes followed the wet, smelly, and shoeless intruders—especially Tuoyo, who was still in her foreman's uniform—down the hallway as they lugged a crate of recycled paper, headed for the nearest freight elevator. A middle-aged woman with streaks of graying hair, riding a small two-seater shaped like an egg, pulled to a stop on the marked track beside them.

"Excuse me—" She was well-dressed, in a patterned kaftan that, in one look, Yekini knew she would never be able to afford unless she moved up here. "Who are you—what are you—"

"OPL business," Ngozi said, putting on the air and voice he had not used since back when they were in level 9.

"Is there a problem?" another passerby said in a hushed tone. "Should we call the police?"

"There is no problem," Ngozi said. "Please, return to your units, and refrain from speaking about what you have seen here until you receive permission to do so."

They went past more perplexed faces, some anxious enough that they made the tiny movements Yekini had seen people often make in a bid for self-preservation—a slight huddling together, an arm about a loved one, the tight grip of a friend's hand. But Ngozi's information seemed to be disseminating with the familiar alacrity of a Midder-level neighborhood, whispered from midder to midder amidst thrilling shivers.

No one bothered them further, though. Not until they were a few feet from the freight elevators, and ran into two armed police personnel.

Tuoyo froze for a split second, and that semi-perceptible shift in countenance was sufficient to trigger the man and woman dressed in red. They turned, their visors immediately dropping over their eyes, scanning the three, hands resting on their firearms as they did so.

"Pinnacle Police," the woman said, speaking through the tinny amplifier that was a part of all police helmets, so that they all sounded like they shared the same robot parent. "State your business."

"Hey, hey," Ngozi said, lifting his hands and stepping forward as Yekini and Tuoyo set the crate aside. The two officers drew their firearms with a swiftness.

"Do not take another step, sir," the man said. "Stay right where you are while we scan, or we will be required to put you down."

"Listen, listen to me," Ngozi said, and Yekini was starting to hear the panic in his voice. "This is an OPL-COPOF operation. We are not required—"

The woman, who seemed to be frowning at the scan results she was seeing in her visor, elbowed her partner, then holstered her weapon. The man did the same.

"Our apologies, sir," she said, her visor retracting to show her face. "We did not know you were a level seventy. I was of the impression you came from the Lowers, when I saw . . ." Her eyes flicked to Tuoyo, and then to Yekini. "Our apologies as well, Agent." She cleared her throat. "Are you cleared to bring this one up here?" She tilted her chin toward Tuoyo.

Yekini's shoulders dropped in relief. "Yes, we are—"

"Who are you calling *this one*?" Tuoyo asked.

Yekini elbowed the engineer and shook her head. *Not now, please.* She returned to the police.

"We are cleared for all activities we're currently carrying out," said Yekini. "But as the OPL official has said, we cannot disclose that information. Feel free to take it up with our people upstairs."

The man eyed her, then put up a finger. "Nobody make a move. I'm going to send up a request."

"At this time of day?" Yekini scoffed. "Good luck getting an answer now. I mean, we're happy to wait until you receive notice of our clearance. But if we have to explain in our report why we didn't get these confidential resources to their due location in time, we'll just have to tell them what happened here. They might want to know your names, too." She squinted for effect, attempting to peer at their projected screen tags. "Officer . . ."

The man pushed a panel and shut off his screen tag. The woman followed suit.

"Wait," said Ngozi. "You're not allowed to do that. You can get suspended for withholding your identity from a towerzen."

The man and woman looked at one another.

"Or," said Yekini, "you can just let us get on our way, and we'll forget this meeting ever happened."

The woman, who looked more agitated, whispered sharply to the man. He gave the trio a nervy gaze.

"Fine, fine," he said. "Carry on."

The woman pushed the freight elevator buttons, and the doors swung open. Yekini and Tuoyo rolled the crate inside. The doors shut.

Or, almost. A red-gloved hand stopped them at the last moment, shoving the doors open. The man and woman were back.

"Our apologies, yet again," the man said, looking contrite. "We should never have pulled our firearms on you."

"Yes, you shouldn't have," said Tuoyo.

"It's fine," said Yekini.

"No, it's not," said the woman. "As a token of our apology, let us escort you and help you get this to where you're going."

"No, we don't need—"

"Oh no," the woman said. "We insist." She nudged her partner. "Right?"

"Right," he said. "We insist."

YEKINI

When Yekini put her wrist to the door of her unit on level 57, she let out a heavy breath long held.

The two police officers had actually helped them. They had encountered more patrols on the way over here, but none had raised an eyebrow, seeing them accompanied by comrades. In fact, the most tenuous part of the trip had been once they'd arrived on the work wing of this level, and the duo bade them goodbye. They had waited for them to disappear before scrambling in the opposite direction, back to the residential wing, and all the way here, where they could finally breathe.

The door slid open, revealing the dimness of the unit, with only the green glow of the clock on the widescreen. The numbers told her it was late evening. A whole day had passed with this ordeal, and it felt like it was only just beginning. But more importantly, she had not set up Maame's evening schedule before she'd left. The woman must be worried sick or completely furious by now, and if she knew her grandmother well, likely both.

Ngozi took a step into the unit, but Yekini held him back.

"Maame?" she called into the dimness. "You there?"

Around the corner from the door came a movement, then sound. A whirring, and soon, Maame's face came around the corner, steering herself in her easy chair. She stopped right before them.

"I'm alone," the woman said.

Yekini let out a big sigh of relief and embraced her grandmother. There was a moment, earlier today, when she had thought she would never see the woman again.

Maame, however, still looked tense, her eyes darting from her granddaughter to the two strangers standing in the unit with her, to the crate they had just brought in. Yekini pulled back and could see her grandmother's finger hovering around the panic button beneath her chair, one that Yekini had installed herself. It was set to directly prompt Yekini's wearable, or to go to her COPOF station up on level 66. And if unanswered, to alert the police.

"Maame, it's okay, you don't need that," she said, gently easing the woman's fingers away. "They are not here to harm us. These are my friends."

"I wasn't going to press it for me," Maame said, then huffed and turned her chair around. "Also, you're late."

Yekini almost laughed. Years on, and the woman still thought herself some kind of super-being. She never used the panic button ever, even when she thought she heard sounds of someone else in the unit, which always turned out to be some sort of appliance undergoing self-cleaning or turning on according to Yekini's settings. They uneased her, these things. But she never used the button. *Of what use is that?* she'd asked, once. *When it's my time, it's my time. I'm not going to fight it.* Of course she'd only wanted to use the button for Yekini's sake.

"Why are they here?" Maame had settled back into her spot, near the big screen, waiting for the countdown toward her favorite program to end and for the program to begin. "They don't belong on this level."

"They're helping me with this," she said, pointing to the crate. "Well, helping us." Yekini and Tuoyo pushed the crate into the unit and set it in the middle of the living area.

"Us, how?" Maame had all but tuned out of the situation.

"Us, as in, the whole tower."

That seemed to bring the woman's attention back. She turned away from the screen completely.

"Maame," Yekini said, pointing to the crate. "I have brought someone I want you to see. I need you to prepare yourself."

Her grandmother narrowed her eyes at the crate, trying to make sense of the whole situation, then decided it was worth it and nodded.

"You can come out," Yekini said aloud.

There was a bang loud enough to startle Yekini herself, but Maame did not seem moved or startled. Another bang, and another, and then the crate fell apart. Rolls of recycled paper came tumbling out. And with them came Omíwálé.

Yekini held her breath.

In the low light and reduced ceiling of the unit, Omíwálé looked even bigger than they had down on level 6. They towered over everyone, but especially Maame, who was sitting.

"Kneel, child," Maame said, somber. "Let me look at you."

Omíwálé obliged, knelt, put their face in front of Yekini's grandmother. Maame put her hands on the Child's cheeks, felt the smoothness of their fish-skin, massaged over their gills. In the silence that ensconced them all, Yekini experienced a true moment of the sublime, her mind racing upon contemplating the vastness of the ocean, the malleability of species, the inadequacy of the concept of humanity, the endless possibilities of being.

Maame kissed Omíwálé's nose. Soft, light.

"All this time," Maame said, "we have waited for you. We have needed you to come, to remind us that we need saving. Thank you." She leaned forward and pressed her forehead into Omíwálé's. "You have risked everything for us. Now, we will risk everything for you."

ASK NOT WHAT IS, BUT WHAT MAY BE

All-Knowing, my friend—

Finally! Isn't it wonderful, when we both inscribe on clouds, and the patterns commingle? How better for the glistening eyes that peek up at us, that the meaning they glean is a useful foretoken. How better for the rain, that it falls sure, convinced of its origin. How better for their Dreams, that the tales of who they are intermingle with tales of who they may become.

A Dream, see, is the past wrapped in the present wrapped in the future.

You know that old tale they tell of a Savior who resurrects after three days in the grave? Now *that* is what you call a Dream: the long tail of hope, of repair, renewal, recovery. A Dream: to revive, reinstate, rehabilitate. Dreams: to rescue, renovate, replace. Dreams upon Dreams: for refreshment, reconstitution, redemption.

Once, we offered stories. Now, it is the time to offer Dreams.

Interlocution; Or, upon Placing the Queen Conch to Ear

Teasing forth the secrets of the Queen Conch requires neither cognition nor sentience. Our foremother offered willingly and freely, and so will the Queen Conch's secrets disseminate. As we once tucked our histories into its body, so will it tuck its stories into ours.

Here, we must pay heed to the Threeness of interlocution. As is the timeless nature of stories, one who peers into the Queen Conch peers into the past, present and future all at once. A body must willingly hold such Threeness if transliteration is to occur. Numbers, letters, symbols, melodies, images, charges, pulses—whatever a body will receive, the Queen Conch gives.

YEKINI

Omíwálé held out a webbed hand. In the cradle of their palm lay the Queen Conch.

There are stories in this world, Omíwálé said. *Bigger than you, than all of us in this room, than this tower, than every Child of Yemoja undersea. Stories of civilizations just like yours and mine, fallen because they could not each recognize a world—worlds, even—beyond themselves. Peoples so limited in thinking that they were happy to be subjected to the slim imagination of a few, if only it offered them safety in a world too big for them to comprehend. But it is not for us to understand the vastness of the world. It is for us to understand our place in it. And that is what all of us—me, my people, everyone on this tower, everyone who has survived this second coming of the waters—need your help with.*

Yekini received the Queen Conch for a second time. It felt less alien this time around, like something that was starting to find a home with her. She felt like a door that had always been open, waiting for the right wind to blow the right person her way, and all she had to do was let them walk through.

This was the ark's keeper, stretching forth their hand. This was her, taking it.

Once, you held this to your ears, Omíwálé was saying. *And it whispered to you the stories within its depths. Now, you must hold it to another kind of ear, one that will take those stories and whisper them to every ear on this tower.*

Omíwálé pointed to the screen in front of them.

"Wait," said Ngozi. "The Queen Conch can speak through . . . screens?"

The Queen Conch tells stories, Omíwálé said, *and stories are not bound by medium. The Queen Conch speaks however it wishes to whomever it wishes, be it you or me, land or sea, natural or artificial.*

It is but a conduit. All we do is listen, and then we may do with its secrets whatever we wish.

Yekini turned to her grandmother then. "Maame."

Her grandmother beckoned for her to kneel, which she did. The old woman smiled through chipped teeth.

"Remember when you complained about being stuck behind the desk," she said. "Remember, I said you did not belong in that agency, but to something greater. Now that purpose has found its way to you. Perhaps it is written somewhere—fate, we call it? Perhaps it is chance. But whatever it is, who am I to interfere?" Maame kissed her forehead. "Go safely, my dear."

Yekini's plan: return to COPOF and sign back in to her station.

It was evening, so the place was going to be empty. She would log in to the system they used to relay key messages to the Uppers. On a regular day, she would speak into the mic and let the software intelligence parse her message and decide, according to its programmed and machine-learned habits, if it was a message to block or intercept, to relay to the Uppers for further processing, or to step aside and allow it to go directly to the announcement system that ran through the tower. The first option she was skilled enough to bypass on her own, but the last two would be up to the Queen Conch.

To achieve this, she would first have to get up to level 66, of course. The elevators were too risky—there were no elevators in residential wings because towerzens were prohibited from moving between levels except for work. Therefore, the only elevators that could take her there were in the opposite wing. They had already gone through there once, and raised enough eyebrows that going back was a sure way to get caught. The elevators could also be halted remotely at any time.

Her only option was something she had more control over: the restricted fire escape stairs.

"That is an *insane* amount of climbing," Ngozi said. "And you're not cleared for stairwell use."

"Yes," she said. "Which is why you're coming with me. You're my override for both levels."

"Coming with—" Ngozi chuckled derisively. "Not even if the Savior comes down and takes my hand. I've done all I can. I've tried."

"So, you're saying your sister would be proud, wouldn't she?" Tuoyo asked. "You're saying you've done everything you can to be worthy of her sacrifice?"

"Don't you even—"

"Even what?" She shook her head. "I've lost someone too, understand? And I would do anything to bring her back. And I can't. But this? This I can do, and I will do, if it's the last thing."

"We don't have time for this," Yekini said. "And that's great, Tuoyo, but I need you for something else. You need to stay here with Maame and Omíwálé."

"Excuse me?"

"The OPL will head here, once they know," she said. "And they *will* know. Someone needs to be here to help these two once they come."

Tuoyo was shaking her head. "I have an even better idea."

"Which is?"

"A diversion." She pointed at Omíwálé. "Let's be frank, Yekini, you know as much as I do that the moment those two scanned us up in sixty-two, it was over. The information that we did not perish in level nine will eventually reach the right screens, and it will only be a matter of time before they come here and take us into custody. They're probably on every camera right now, trying to identify us. The moment you step out that door, you will not get up one level before they box you in."

"I can try. We can be quick, we'll—"

Tuoyo put a hand on Yekini's shoulder. "It's fine. I'm not afraid. And I don't think Omíwálé is either." She looked to the Child. "Are you?"

The Child shook their head.

"See?" Tuoyo allowed herself a small smile. "None of us is new to sacrifice. We have made sacrifices every day just to exist as we are on this tower. We made a sacrifice when we survived level nine, made a sacrifice the moment we all decided not to bind Omíwálé and turn them in to the OPL. What is there in one more sacrifice, especially one with the possibility of opening us all to the truth of who we are and what we've done, of setting us free?"

Silence engulfed the unit, the weight of Tuoyo's words pressing down on them all. A beep went on somewhere, and the unit assistant sent a kettle clattering, filling it with water and setting it to boil.

Omíwálé made a sound, like a chuckle, which came out more like a gurgle.

There was always the risk of being caught and contained, they said. *Either by my people or yours, and before I got to finish my task of telling these stories. Perhaps now is as good a time as any.*

They turned to look at Tuoyo. *I will go with you,* they said.

Yekini eyed both, then nodded. "Okay."

"We go first," Tuoyo said, breaking it all down. She would leave with Omíwálé, ensuring that they were seen by both cameras and eyes. Calls would flood in to the police. There would be mayhem, and within that mayhem, Yekini and Ngozi, in new clothes and disguises, could slip into the stairwell and begin their ascent.

"And you two?"

"Don't worry about us," Tuoyo said. "We can make it hard for them." She chuckled. "They should've never let us both— one who can find their way around this tower pretty easily, and one who can knock their way into walls—find our way to each other." She winked at Omíwálé. The Child responded with what Yekini thought was a grimace. She turned to Ngozi.

"Now, you're my only chance," she said. "Do this, and this will be the last thing you ever have to do for us, I promise."

Ngozi shut his eyes, and for a moment, looked like he was praying. But he was murmuring something, instead, and when Yekini listened closely, she could make out the words. *Make it count,* he was saying. *Make it count.*

Finally, he opened his eyes. "I'm not doing it for you," he said.

Yekini kissed Maame on the forehead. "Will you be okay? When they come?"

"What they going to do with an old woman in an easy chair?" She scoffed. "You all go. I'll be fine."

Yekini regarded the people before her, putting their lives on the line to bring truth to the tower, to the world. These were her babies in a basket. She might have let them down many times before, when she didn't understand. But that was before. Today—today was going to be different.

TUOYO

Ngozi and Yekini got out of their smelly work clothes and dressed in new garments. When they emerged from the inner room, they looked like complete strangers, separate from the two people Tuoyo had just spent hours in the doldrums with. Flamboyant kaftans, muted enough to not be easily noticeable in a crowd, colorful enough to demonstrate the owner's penchant for quiet rebellion, little pieces of themselves sewn into the fabric.

"My husband's," Maame said, when she saw Tuoyo's inspecting gaze. "Then hers after." She tilted her chin toward Yekini. "Re-made in our image, she and clothes both, eh?"

Tuoyo offered a wry smile. Maame looked her up and down.

"You will need to let it go, you hear? Or at least use it for something good."

"What?"

"The anger, the pain, the quest for self-destruction," she said. "If you're going to use it, use it for something good. Don't self-combust for nothing."

Tuoyo decided she didn't know what the old woman was talking about, but as she watched Yekini snap the magnetic buttons of Ngozi's kaftan into place, it settled upon her. She had tried to run away from it—from all of this—but it had found her anyway. To walk away from it now would be a waste, wouldn't it?

Omíwálé was to be covered in a large bedsheet, to be revealed at the proper time to cause the right kind of distraction. The Child put it on, and was instantly transformed into a ghostly, spiritual character. A god, even, if Tuoyo tilted her head the right way.

Then it was time to take the most important step: to demand that the world look.

"How do you feel about this?" Tuoyo asked Omíwálé. "I understand if you have cold feet. Well, you probably always have those, isn't it?" She chuckled at the joke.

I have wanted nothing but to be seen, Omíwálé said from beneath the sheet. *I welcome it. And I welcome that you make jokes of it.*

"Are you going to say anything?" Yekini asked. "While out there?"

"Maybe," Tuoyo said, looking to the ceiling. "It'll come to me."

Then she opened the door a slice, peeked through, and slipped out with the Child behind her.

When the first cameras caught the image of them, Tuoyo expected the response to be immediate, like it had been down in level 9. Instead, it was a different kind of camera—the eyes of the first of Yekini's neighbors on level 57—that registered them and raised questions.

"Who are you?" a woman, who had just opened her door, then wrinkled her nose in the air, said. "And what's that smell you bring with you?" Her eyes shifted to the tall person with a white sheet draped over them, trying to make sense of what she was seeing. But Tuoyo did just as planned—she kept it moving.

"Excuse me, I'm talking to—" There was a quiver beneath the woman's voice. "Should you be on this level?"

"Mama?" A little girl, who could not have been more than six, appeared next to the woman, holding on to her legs. "Mama—what is that?"

Tuoyo looked the young child over. There was no disdain or hate in her gaze or question, nothing but inquiry and interest, nothing but a desire to understand and make sense of the world around her.

She winked at the girl. This was who she was doing this for. The time left between moving from this impressionable little girl to this older, misinformed mother was closing with every second. Tuoyo felt it, the responsibility she had been given, a chance to stop that growth now before it was too late.

So, in the middle of the residential hallway of level 57, Tuoyo pulled down the bedsheet and revealed the Child.

"Go tap your daddy," the woman said, pushing the girl back into the doorway with a trembling arm, her eyes wide as saucers. "Tell him to ping the police."

OFFICE OF THE PINNACLE LEADERSHIP
SOCIOLOGICAL RESEARCH REPORT

Start of excerpt.

File Metadata

Class: DECLASSIFIED

Tower: PINNACLE

Subject: Understanding ~~the Health Risks of~~ Confined Spaces

Date: DAY 179, YEAR 001

Summary: How may living in the ~~small and confined spaces of the~~ Fingers impact ~~the psychological health and behavior of~~ its residents?

Report by: Cynthia Orun, Architect and Lead Researcher

Note: This file has been cleared for external use and distribution.

The housing needs for an average resident of the Fingers are minimal: privacy, security, sleeping and living areas. These are easily accomplished within the ~~modest~~ space available in each tower's assigned living units. ~~But our studies of how community functions in confined spaces suggests that is only half the picture.~~

In past reports, we have noted how ~~the lack of windows in most~~ middle units, for instance, ~~have direct ties to tower residents feeling overcrowded despite being believed to~~ offer spatial sufficiency. ~~This feeling has then been linked to an uptick in social withdrawal, stress, and aggression among tower dwellers.~~

Current research reveals that each tower, over time, has formulated its own ~~artificial~~ bionomics, psychological ecology and rhythm. ~~This evolution has resulted in the collision of various coping mechanisms and mental anxieties of living in such a confined space for a long time. We have linked to this phenomenon upticks in insomnia; addiction to alcohol, drugs and sex; and an overwhelming penchant for aggression.~~

End of excerpt.

TUⓞYⓞ

Tuoyo did not run.

She had not been completely forthcoming to Yekini and the rest of the group about what would happen next after they had been seen and caused the diversion. Contrary to what she had told the group, her time spent between the Midders and the Lowers had not actually equipped her to understand the Pinnacle's walls and how to hide within them. In fact, she had no plans at all for what she and Omíwálé would do after revealing themselves. She had left out one key fact, hoping no one would ask: she and Omíwálé could not leave level 57. As a lower, she was not authorized for this level, and therefore could not move around freely or override anything, especially with a Child in tow.

In fact, she had asked to do this for a very specific reason: to see the sea at night one last time.

Once they had gotten enough unit doors open, Tuoyo led Omíwálé down the rest of the residential wing before the crowd got too large to pass through. At the end of the hallway, she took the conveyor, the only thing that did not require her to prove that she belonged on this level. It took her and Omíwálé away from the now crowded residential wing, away from the emptier-at-this-time-of-day administrative and maintenance wings, and dropped them off at the level-wide concourse.

One side of the concourse was stacked from top to bottom with cubicles that acted as trading shops, where certified traders sold goods imported from both the lower and upper levels that people were prohibited from visiting. They stood neck-to-neck with department stores, pharmacies, beauty shops, a few restaurants. Most were closed at this time, with some just rounding off, and a few, like the sole nightclub of the lot, were still going.

The other side of the concourse, which Tuoyo headed for with Omíwálé, sported a lengthy series of expansive windows, screed-to-ceiling glass lookouts that offered a view of the sparkling sea at dusk, haloed by the glow of an early moon. Tuoyo and Omíwálé climbed the steps and stood at the railing, completely oblivious to the chaos in their wake: customers and workers and security personnel alike, each, upon sighting the Child, devolving into the most basic human responses after perceiving something deemed monstrous: fright, flight, fight. Luckily, none made it past the first two responses into the third. In a matter of seconds, the immediate area about the two visitors was cleared, and Tuoyo could enjoy the sight in the silence she deserved.

"I used to stand at a window just like this with my wife," she said to Omíwálé, who was not as oblivious to the events around them, but remained just as calm. "Back when we were still here, in the Midders. We'd look out and talk about what our future might look like." She smirked. "You think she's still out there right now?"

No, Omíwálé replied. *But in your memory, she remains.* The Child tapped her temple with a webbed finger. *The key is never to forget. Memory must be kept alive. It helps us understand our past, situate ourselves in the present and position ourselves for the future.*

"Yeah," Tuoyo said. "I get that now." She gazed up at the Child. "For so long, I hated you—the idea of others like you. But it was never you, you know? I lost my anchor, the person I felt was most worth living for. I hated myself for losing control, for letting the OPL push me around like boiled vegetables on a child's plate. And I was most angry that I believed they were right, that it was in service of the greater good for me to shrink." She sighed. "But this—all of this today—is the most alive I've ever felt since . . . her. And if this is the way I go down, then so be it." She rested an apologetic hand on the Child's scaly upper arm. "And I apologize— for not telling you before."

That we would be caught? Omíwálé managed what Tuoyo considered to be a smile. *That, I already knew.*

From far away, the sounds of activity came. Time as a lower had made Tuoyo familiar with the sounds of resistance, as well as the sounds of that which came to suffocate it. The sounds she heard now—the feedback of an announcement system getting ready to be deployed, weaponry undocked and leveled, a smothering force advancing, moving like a palm over mouth—she recognized them all.

I have a family, do you know? Omíwálé was saying. *I could not bring them with me, because I did not know if I would survive. But I knew: if the distance of time and space and knowledge between both our peoples must be breached, then we must understand each other, and the only way to do that is to look into who we are, who we have always been—to let the Queen Conch tell our stories. Taking the Queen Conch was a betrayal of my people, but a worthy one. It cost me everything I have ever known. On my journey here, I wondered if I had done the right thing. But if this is any indication, I know I have at least made a noble attempt, one that, if fruitful, could save future generations from dying in wars and disputes.*

Omíwálé turned and held out their arms, signaling to the advancing sea of red berets and uniforms and weapons that they meant no harm. Tuoyo turned, her back to the moon, and held out her hands in similar fashion, surrendering.

We are but messengers, Omíwálé said to Tuoyo. *Every once in a while, we perish at the mercy of the weighty stories we carry. But sometimes—sometimes, we prevail, and the stories we carry change the world.*

The Pinnacle Police Force ascended the steps to the balustrade, their helmets and visors commingling into one red wave, swallowing everything they touched.

YEKINI

In her nearly thirty years of living on this tower, Yekini had never experienced a riot. As far as she knew, there had only been two riots in the Pinnacle's history. One of them had happened in the Lowers, and from what she'd learned, the inhabitants of various levels had insisted on being freed from their labor and let out of the tower. After refusing to work, destroying useful infrastructure and equipment in their rage, and putting the fate of the whole tower in peril as a result, the rioters forced the OPL to let them out. They were ferried up to the surface, put on boats, and shipped out to sea, where it didn't take long before they were swallowed up, never to be seen again.

After today, though, Yekini strongly doubted the veracity of those reports.

The second riot had happened right here, in the Midders. It was spoken about less, the details fuzzier. It was unclear what midders would have to riot about, though Yekini had a theory. The Pinnacle was a metal container, and its inhabitants were cockroaches captured and bottled up inside it. No matter how good any of them had it, it was only a matter of time before they would become erratic, strained, stretched taut to the limits of their sanity.

That was what she banked upon, letting Tuoyo and Omíwálé walk out that door. And she was rewarded when the first strains of noise and chatter from the hallway began to filter into the unit.

"Time to go," she said to Ngozi, and they slipped out the door.

A crowd bigger than she'd ever seen on this level filled the hallway. It was less a crowd and more a milling of people chatting about what someone had reported seeing. Unit doors stood open and families—children, spouses, siblings, grandparents—filtered in and out, chattering, many in leisurewear that showed they had been in the middle of various activities. They gathered in a buzz, exchanging everything from simple gossip to conspiracy theories.

"They say it was ten feet tall," someone whispered, "and that it came from the sea."

"They say it can fly," another said. "That's how it was able to get so high up into this level."

"I hear it's working with a lower, who brought it up here," a third offered. "You know how I've been saying those lowers will be the death of us all?"

Yekini had Ngozi in front of her as they weaved through the crowd silently, the Queen Conch tucked beneath her kaftan. They moved like snakes parting grass, as she'd seen in the old wildlife programs. She'd seen many a great thing too, in those archives, a lot of them she was locked out of even as a COPOF analyst. She wondered how much the average resident was being locked out of.

Down the hallway, and thankfully in the direction opposite to where they were headed, a fracas had broken out. Many pounded on elevator doors, some shouting into cameras, asking that the OPL provide explanation. The doors themselves had opened, and the red berets of tower police appeared behind the crowd. A message began to play on the intercom that Yekini couldn't quite hear over the noise. The announcement and advertisement screens had begun to come alive too. Soon the Pinnacle prime's face would be plastered all over them, calling for calm, asking them to aid police in finding the Child, and asking them to turn over the traitors in their midst.

When she was through, though, that would matter little. The searing truths she had witnessed when she placed the Queen Conch as instructed, and tapped into its endless depth of knowledge in one fell swoop: that was something she could never be locked out of. And Savior willing, every resident of this tower would soon be able to tap into that greatness and witness these truths—about themselves, and about the Children.

They arrived at the door to the stairs. Ngozi held his forearm to it and offered the required scan for override. The door opened into the dimly lit staircase. Yekini stepped forward and did not look back: at the screens, at the chaos in her wake, at the people she may possibly never see again.

NGOZI

The Midder stairs of the Pinnacle were not really built for climbing, mostly because they were barely ever climbed. They were there for emergencies, for when the elevators broke down and workers needed to get from place to place. It took Ngozi just the first flight to realize that not only was he not built for this experience, it wasn't built for him either.

"What in the Savior's waters . . ." he cursed, then paused for breath, hands on his knees. "How much farther?"

"We've only gone up three," Yekini said. "Five more. Come on, they'll find us soon."

He sucked in a breath that stung his airway and his belly, then started up again. Yekini seemed to have done this a lot more often than he, who had never been back here. Well, except once, when he was a child and too young to remember. Apparently, Lota had had to carry him as they were smuggled into the tower. The groups that brought in refugees or illegals born in floating settlements outside the Pinnacle always kept them moving. Stairs were an efficient pathway to survival, it seemed, but also revolution. Without these stairs, he wouldn't even be alive.

They went up one flight and then another. The stairs were wide enough, but the dimness of the stairwell made him uncomfortable. Just like with down at level 6, it reminded him of his time spent packed with other illegals, stuffed into one new unit after another, lights off, living in the darkness so as not to attract undue attention. Sometimes, when their handlers got found out, they were split and scattered, sent to new handlers, who stuffed them in just-as-dark closets. All of this, Lota told him, of course. He'd been too young to remember the events, though not too young to remember the feelings. That period of his life, he'd chalked up to one long nightmare he'd never revisit. Until today, that was.

They went up another flight.

You would be proud, he thought, touching his necklace. *You would approve.*

It didn't take long for the first sign of trouble to show up.

Right when they were on the stairs of the penultimate level—65—a door below them opened up. Ngozi looked down, over the railings, and saw a red beret staring back up at him, three or so levels down.

"They're here!" the voice said, perhaps into an earcomm, their voice echoing in the stairwell. Then the person pulled out a firearm and trained it in Ngozi's direction. "Police! Stop where you are, in the name of the prime—"

Ngozi and Yekini ran the rest of the way.

The first shot didn't come immediately, almost like the police personnel still hoped they would follow their commands. But Ngozi knew that was moot—giving over now was the worst possible scenario. There was no way he was ever going back to work for the OPL, and whatever the outcome of this, his life on this tower was over. Over, maybe, but not completely useless. It may have taken him this long, but with today's events, he had finally arrived at his eureka moment.

His greatest fear was not loss. It was uselessness.

Make it count, Lota had said. And that was exactly what he was going to do.

They were a few steps from the stairwell entrance to 66 when the first bullet whizzed past Ngozi and struck the wall. Another struck the metal banister, only a foot away. Yekini ducked, pulling her own weapon and firing back to buy them time.

He took that time to focus on his task, placing his forearm to the stairwell panel and completing the biometric tests. The door jammed open. He pulled it and ushered Yekini forward hastily. The shouts were getting louder now, as more doors below them opened, and more police poured into the stairwell, yelling the same command over and over, like programmed robots. *Stop in the name of the prime!*

Yekini stopped firing and ran through the door. She had

taken a few steps before she looked back and realized what was happening.

"What are you doing?" she yelled, but he didn't listen. He pushed the door closed as she banged on it from the other side. He placed a hand on the glass panel and nodded.

"Go," he said, even though he knew she could not hear him. "Make it count."

Then he jammed his elbow into the door panel and shattered it.

When the sea of red uniforms and berets reached for him, hands pinning him down as one, his nose in the cold of the floor, he closed his eyes and thought of Lota: sent back to sea, to the floating community from which she had come, back into the unforgiving waves. He wondered if she made it out—whether as a human from oversea, or as a Child from undersea. He wondered if she and Omíwálé were the same, now. He wondered, as they put a hood over his head to blindfold him, if, as she had given herself up so he may have life, he was doing the same for her too.

Revelation; Or, upon Placing the Queen Conch to Heart

Blessed is the eye that gazes within, that looks past the fear and unearths the self. Blessed is the eye that stares into the dark, to find home there.

Blessed is the arm that lays itself down on altar, that severs itself, lest it brings a body to sin.

Blessed are the lips that speak truth and the tongues that aid them. Blessed are the teeth that gate falsehoods, that bite, that reprimand the errant mouth.

Blessed are the limbs that carry the messengers—four or two or one or none. Blessed are the messages carried.

Blessed is the heart that bears no judgment, that walks across time and space with its doors open, that brings life to holder and beholder both. Blessed is the revelation it carries, the awakening it brings, the light it shares. Blessed is the fruit of its labor, the future that spills forth.

Blessed is the time and space between existences, and the hearts that bridge them.

YEKINI

At some point during her time on level 9, Yekini had wondered how the day would end. Never had she imagined it would happen at the same place it all began. The grid of workstations, still there when she turned on the lights, now empty and sterile under the hum of illumination.

She ran to her workzone, turned on her station, and pulled the command mic to herself. She ran her fingers over the slippery smoothness of the Queen Conch one last time, placed it on the desk, tunnel face-up, and pointed the camera and command mic to it.

Then she sat down and waited.

How long she sat there before it all went down would later become a matter of debate. Reports would say a few minutes, others would say at least an hour, and a few more would go on to say it was only a few seconds. Yekini herself would find it difficult to remember anything about time. Perhaps because, in that moment, she existed in a bubble of timelessness. Everything and nothing ran through her mind, and other than stare at the Queen Conch and the command access point that was pointed at it in the form of a camera and mic, she did nothing but wish.

She wished to let go.

When the sea of red berets and uniforms finally arrived, filing into the COPOF workzones, slipping behind barriers and uttering commands that she could not hear, absolutely nothing had happened with the Queen Conch. Or at least, so she believed. But something within her *knew,* and it gave her the fortitude to press her thumb to her station and offer the software intelligence the command she needed to.

"Activate emergency lock systems," she said.

Are you sure? the software asked.

Yes, thought Yekini. *Yes I am.*

The lights in the room changed to a swift red, and the glass doors and walls that separated her workzone from the others froze into their preprogrammed thickness—fireproof, water-proof, weapon-proof. The red berets and the smattering of CO-POF officers within them—Yekini could almost swear she could see Monsignor and Director Merit Timipre among them—rushed to the doors once they knew what was happening. But it was too late—they were locked out.

There was a momentary pause in the tumult, then someone began to hack at the glass with something heavy.

Yekini relaxed into her chair and called up views from cam-eras around the tower. In the hallway of level 57, right outside her unit, Maame was being rolled out by staff from Health Ser-vices. Next to her was Tuoyo, already secured by the red berets, Maame being asked to identify her. Omíwálé was nowhere to be seen, but Yekini already knew that whatever had happened to them—whether they had escaped, been taken away, or pres-ent but invisible to the camera's eye—she would never see them again.

In the stairwell of level 66, she saw Ngozi secured, dragged into a corner. He looked alive and well, not at all like the righ-teously mad person she had spent most of the time on level 9 with, but a person satisfied, a mad grin plastered all over his face before a bag was placed over his head.

The cameras on level 9 were locked to her, and she did not have the time and energy to attempt a hack right now, not with that thudding on the glass by the police. So she let herself imag-ine instead, wondering where the bodies would go after floating and bloating, wondering if they would be flushed out to sea or just left there to rot until they were cleared away for some new project—maybe a new agricultural level?

But she didn't need to tell that story to the whole tower, now. The Queen Conch was right there, holder of histories, a mouth for the gagged. Back at the unit, while they waited, she had whis-pered the story of everything to the Queen Conch: of the fate of level 9 and its inhabitants; of Tuoyo and Nehikhare; of Ngozi and Lota; of Omíwálé and their sacrifice; of the Pinnacle's deadly creed. She had asked the Queen Conch and the foremother from whom it came, Yemoja, to keep safe this story. Not just for her Children who came from undersea, but for her children oversea as well, who needed her help just as much.

Now, she had freed the Queen Conch, and wished for it to do its job.

Right before the containment glass finally shattered under the force of the police's attack, Yekini believed she saw something in the cameras. Not a glitch, because her eyes wouldn't deceive her so. More like an actual freeze in time, where everyone paused for a hair between moments, as something new arrived in their consciousness. Something true and weighty and larger-than-life. Something akin to the myriad of feelings and experiences and understanding she had gained upon putting the Queen Conch, as instructed, to eye, to skin, to nose, to lips, to ear.

Something began to appear across every form of media—screen, audio, text—taking over her workstation, commandeering. Yekini leaned forward in her chair, the approaching boots on glass and screaming commands and weapons coming closer and closer.

She would never know, because the sea of red about her rose, without warning, and enveloped her. The images on her workstation drifted away like an ark, floating off with all the answers. But she feared not where it would go, because her heart had found rest—for when she looked down in her hand, there was no basket in it.

ACKNOWLEDGMENTS

What are you but angels in disguise?

Thank you—

—**Jonathan Strahan,** for soliciting this manuscript and helping shape and shepherd it to the place it now occupies in the world; **Eli Goldman,** for delighting in my stories long before this one, and unabashedly making that delight known; copy editor **Christina MacDonald,** cover artist **Raphael Lacoste,** art director **Christine Foltzer,** and the rest of the team at **Tordotcom** and beyond;

—**Chris Cokinos,** for supervising this manuscript during my MFA at the University of Arizona; for forcing me to ask deeper questions about its aims and influences; for assuaging my fear of writing anything in stanzas;

—**Tade Thompson,** for your early critique of this work, for your notes on orality, and for your unwavering support over the years; **Aurelie Sheehan,** for offering to be the final tentpole in my thesis committee, for your kind and careful critique, and for being one of the most thoughtful personalities I've had the honor of working with—rest in peace;

—**Kate Bernheimer,** and fellow grads who first provided feedback for this story back in 2019: **Lucia Edafioka, Kim Bussing, Joi Massat, Samiha Matin, Brian Randall; Bojan Louis,** for the Indigenous poetics class that got me thinking deeply about poetry and place; **Julie Iromuanya,** for being a support system during my early days in Tucson;

—**Logan Phillips** and **Gabriel Dozal,** Tucson poets I deeply respect, who taught me how to break a line and give rhythm to sentences; **Lucy Kirkman,** who encouraged me to write poetry in the first place: you were a light—rest in peace;

—The Center for Science and the Imagination at ASU, particularly **Ed Finn,** for being open to a chat after only a cold email, and **Joey Eschrich,** for reaching out with one new opportunity after another, and encouraging me to take each;

—**Tamara Kawar** (and the DeFiore & Company team) and **Alexander Cochran** (and the C&W team), for being steadfast stewards of my writing career;

—D, as always, for putting up with me; and the lil' youngling, for reminding me that little doesn't always mean insignificant;

—The libraries at the University of Arizona and the University of Ottawa, for providing me with the source materials that fueled and buttressed this story; and the authors of said works, particularly: Rita Indiana, for *Tentacle;* J. G. Ballard, for *High-Rise;* Jacques Lob, for *Le Transperceneige* (*Snowpiercer*); Gabriel Okara, for *The Fisherman's Invocation* and other poems; Rivers Solomon, Daveed Diggs, William Hutson, and Jonathan Snipes, for *The Deep;* Grace Dillon, for curating *Walking the Clouds;* Anthony Aveni, for *Creation Stories;* James George Frazer, for "Ancient Stories of a Great Flood"; William Baker, for "The Future of Tall Building Technology"; *The What If Show,* for episodes on living underwater;

—Every reader out there who has engaged with my stories and helped others find them one way or another: You are the reason I do what I do. I appreciate you.

ABOUT THE AUTHOR

Photo credit: Manuel Ruiz

SUYI DAVIES OKUNGBOWA is an author of fantasy, science fiction, and general speculative work. His latest novel is *Son of the Storm,* first in the epic fantasy trilogy The Nameless Republic. His debut godpunk fantasy novel, *David Mogo, Godhunter,* won the 2020 Ilube Nommo Award for Best Speculative Fiction Novel by an African. His shorter works have appeared in various periodicals and anthologies and have been nominated for various awards. He earned his MFA in creative writing at the University of Arizona and currently teaches at the University of Ottawa.

suyidavies.com
Instagram: @suyidavies
Bluesky: @suyidavies.com
TikTok: @suyidavies